The Beekeeper's Secret

What others are saying about *The Beekeeper's Secret...*

"Twists and turns abound as Fernandez precisely knits facts with imagination to entertain and to educate in a genuine page-turner too irresistible to put down."

—Michael DeStefano, Award-winning Author of *The Composer's Legacy*

"Relentless tenacity couples with a 'Never Give In; Never Give Up' attitude, driving Max to detective stardom. The same intrepid attitude that got us to the Moon and back permeates this heroine's achievement!!! The reader gets into multiple missions and locations, absorbing each challenge connecting new dimensions of intrigue wrapped in skullduggery! Prepare to get launched into spatial excitement!!!"

—Tom Wysmuller, NASA Apollo Era (Ret.), VP Medical Claims Operations, Phoenix Mutual Life Insurance Company (Former)

"Sally Fernandez has written a fascinating novel, which revolves around the honey bee and the beekeepers who are working hard to keep them alive and healthy. Even though this book is a work of fiction, it is intertwined with a great deal of factual information about honey bees."

—Gene Brandi, Gene Brandi Apiaries, Past President of American Beekeeping Federation

"Max Ford is a wonderful character brought to life in all her glory by Sally Fernandez, an author who weaves intrigue, mystery, drama, and lighthearted repartee into a well researched book which addresses an issue that impacts all of us. *The Beekeeper's Secret* is a must-read—a fast read—and a read I would strongly recommend."

—Donna Post, Banking Consultant (Ret.)

"As an alternative practitioner, I am thrilled to see this book available. Knowing some of the people involved, I am looking forward to reading and sharing *The Beekeeper's Secret*."

—Dr. Michele Benoit, Chiropractor

"Again, I am astonished by a Fernandez thriller with such amazing and authentic research that keeps my mind reeling with suspense while continuing to be educated. As a devotee of alternative medicine and a lover of nature, *The Beekeeper's Secret* must be revealed."

—Kenney DeCamp, Physician Assistant, Chef, Producer, Mime

"Another eye-opener with dangerous consequences. Max Ford does it again, using her tenaciousness to shine a light on the self-serving manipulation from those who espouse to protect us. Max exposes how our freedom of choice is being sacrificed in the name of greed. This book should have been written long ago, but better late than never, because you will not want to put it down."

—Ann E. Howells, Wine Consultant

"The fun thing about reading thriller-mysteries or mystery-thrillers is connecting the dots. A good storyteller keeps you guessing with bits and pieces of plot line that don't seem connected, and then drops in a hint that sets you off in the right direction and then surprises you with yet another turn. As in her earlier novels, Sally Fernandez does it again with *The Beekeeper's Secret* — a crisp, fast read built on intriguing, clever, contemporary issues that make you think a lot, with a dash of humor here and there."

—Alfredo S. Vedro, Media Production Consultant

The Beekeeper's Secret

A Max Ford Thriller

A NOVEL

SALLY FERNANDEZ

DUNHAM
books

The Beekeeper's Secret
A Max Ford Thriller
Copyright © 2018 by Sally Fernandez

Trade Paperback ISBN: 9780999664629

eBook ISBN: 9780999664636

Library of Congress Control Number: 2018935062

Printed in the United States of America

Dedicated to David Dunham,
my publisher and dear friend, who by the grace of God
won the battle against pancreatic cancer.
The path David chose became the inspiration for this story.

"Let food be thy medicine and medicine be thy food."
~ Hippocrates (460-370BC)

"The doctor of the future will no longer treat the human frame with drugs, but rather will cure and prevent disease with nutrition."
~ Thomas Edison (1847-1931)

"Many cancer patients use complementary and alternative medicines. Oncologists therefore need to learn more about this subject."
~ E. Ernst, Professor of Complementary Medicine, The Lancet (2000)

"What an extraordinary achievement for a civilization: to have developed the one diet that reliably makes its people sick!"
~ Michael Pollan, *Food Rules: An Eater's Manual* (2009)

"They may have salt, sugar, and fat on their side, but we, ultimately, have the power to make choices. After all, we decide what to buy. We decide how much to eat."
~ Michael Moss, *Salt Sugar Fat: How the Food Giants Hooked Us* (2013)

"In 2017, there will be an estimated 1,688,780 new cancer cases diagnosed and 600,920 cancer deaths in the U.S."
~ American Cancer Society, Annual Report (2017)

LEGION OF CHARACTERS

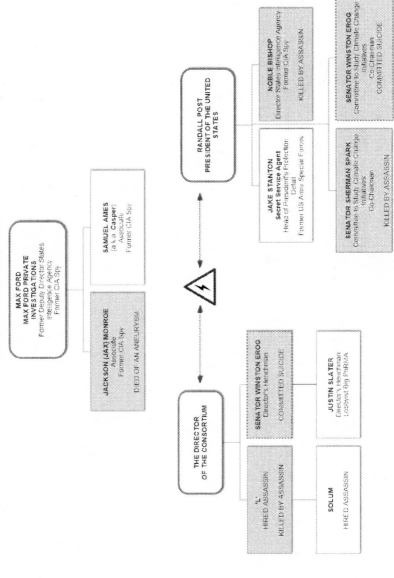

MAX FORD
MAX FORD PRIVATE
INVESTIGATIONS
Former Deputy Director States
Intelligence Agency
Former CIA Spy

JACKSON (JAX) MONROE
Associate
Former CIA Spy

DIED OF AN ANEURYSM

SAMUEL AMES
(a.k.a Casper)
Associate
Former CIA Spy

THE DIRECTOR
OF THE CONSORTIUM

SENATOR WINSTON EROG
Director's Henchman
COMMITTED SUICIDE

JUSTIN SLATER
Director's Henchman
Lobbyist Big PHRMA

"L"
HIRED ASSASSIN
KILLED BY ASSASSIN

SOLUM
HIRED ASSASSIN

RANDALL POST
PRESIDENT OF THE UNITED
STATES

JAKE STANTON
Secret Service Agent
Head of President's Protection
Detail
Former US Army Special Forces

NOBLE BISHOP
Director States Intelligence Agency
Former CIA Spy
KILLED BY ASSASSIN

SENATOR SHERMAN SPARK
Committee to Study Climate Change
Initiatives
Co-Chairman
KILLED BY ASSASSIN

SENATOR WINSTON EROG
Committee to Study Climate Change
Initiatives
Co-Chairman
COMMITTED SUICIDE

Chapter 1

Meet The Macumba

Jeff's stomach was roiling with agita; another plane, another trip, nothing unusual—except this time it will be different.

"Here you are," Allison said, startling him as he was deep in thought. She noticed something was worrying him as she handed him a stack of neatly ironed, impeccably folded shirts. "Are you okay?"

"Thanks. I'm fine." He ignored her concern and placed the shirts in his luggage. At the same time, he noticed a FOX News Alert pop up on the TV screen. "Will you turn up the volume?" he asked.

"We have breaking news," said the staff reporter from the KPTV FOX News Affiliate. "'The death of a Gresham woman in Lincoln City has been ruled a drowning and foul play is not suspected, according to police. Jeana Beck was reported missing late last week. Investigators said she was visiting the Oregon coast with her 23-year old autistic son and did not return after leaving their motel room to have a cigarette Thursday night. Her body was found Friday night in a canal that runs behind the Rodeway Inn & Suites on the 1000 block of Southeast 1st Street in Lincoln City.'"

"How tragic," Allison injected.

"Shh!"

"'...The Oregon State Medical Examiner's Office conducted an autopsy and Beck's probable cause of death was determined to be drowning,'" the reporter confirmed.

Jeff's head was spinning. *How many does that make now, 70, 80? When does it stop?* Thoughts he could not shake.

"What's wrong?" Allison noticed the alarmed expression on his face.

"Nothing. I've got to get going or I'll miss my flight."

The Norwegian appeared out of place, there in the heart of the Amazon, as he sat in the sparsely decorated lobby of the Seringal Hotel. It was not long before the desk clerk on duty became suspicious of the man in the tattered khakis with aging blond hair and roving blue eyes. Most worrisome were the stranger's obsessive facial movements that waltzed between the wall clock and the elevator. After twenty minutes of observing this compulsive behavior, the desk clerk opted to intervene. As he was about to approach, the stranger shot upright without warning, startling the clerk, and accentuating his lofty stature.

Across the lobby, in the other direction, appeared another man in stark contrast, dressed in dark pants and a white business shirt with the sleeves rolled up. He had just dropped off his room key at the front desk before heading in the stranger's direction. Seeing this interplay, the desk clerk retreated to his post, passing the new hotel guest on his way.

The Norwegian checked his phone. The man walking toward him matched the figure in the photo to a T. "You're late," he blurted out to the man he knew was Senator Jeffrey Lance. "I've been waiting for over a half hour." He did not mean to display such agitation, but they were on a mission with a tight schedule.

"Caught up on a conference call," Lance replied. He made no attempt to hide his distress after a lengthy and exhausting flight and a restless night. "So—you're Sorenson?"

"Yes, and welcome to Manaus. Hey, sorry for the slight outburst, but we have less than six hours to get in and out before sundown."

"Then let's go!"

Sorenson eyed the senator from head to toe. "Change your clothes. It gets miserably uncomfortable where we're going. And cover up as much as possible."

Lance's day had already spanned over twenty-four hours. It had been a mad rush from the beginning to the end, starting with fielding several calls and signing a massive stack of documents, before leaving his office. Then, he fought traffic all the way to Reagan National, almost missing the dreaded connection in Miami to board his flight to Manaus, Brazil. The inability to sleep only added to his woes. No thought was given to a choice of clothing until the moment Sorenson pointed out the obvious. At that moment, Lance itched to get into something more fitting for the climate. "Give me five."

"We're heading into *Malariaville!*" Sorenson called out, as Lance dashed back to the front desk to fetch his key again. While anxiously waiting, he tried to recall the last time he had had a vaccine for anything. *I'm sure I had shots sometime within the last three months,* he prayed. Lance grabbed his room key from the desk clerk, and he rushed to the staircase, not waiting for the elevator.

The local time was half past eleven on a late December morning. The sun was already sizzling above, radiating temperatures in the high nineties, with eighty-five-percent humidity saturating the air. And the inadequate air conditioner in Sorenson's Hummer only added to the full-body assault.

"How long before we arrive?" Lance asked, not having a clue as to their destination. Others had planned the trip; he was only privy to one leg at a time. His only choice was to contend with the magical mystery tour.

"Another half hour, after one stop," Sorenson mumbled.

"Stop where?" Lance tried again to eke out a clue.

Sorenson was not playing along.

They had only been on the road for a little over twenty minutes, but it seemed like an hour as Sorenson weaved in and out of the traffic in Manaus. During that time, Lance discovered that his new mate was a man of few words and a despiser of small talk. But Lance goaded him into talking about the city to help fill the vacuum of time.

"If you insist," Sorenson sighed before he began his travelogue. "I'm sure you know that because of Manaus's location, the ship construction industry thrived and allowed for the export of a wide range of goods. But you may not know that the merging of rivers that made this possible is referred to as 'Meeting of the Waters.'"

Lance was well versed, and his prodding was only an exercise to refute boredom. From his past trips to Brazil, he learned that Manaus was the capital city of the state of Amazonas and that it was in the heart of the Amazon rainforest. He also knew the city is ideally perched between the Rio Negro and the Solimões River that converge to become the Amazon River. As Sorenson droned on, Lance continued to half-listen while he focused on the activity swarming outside his window. The Manaus' traffic was reminiscent of the bridge and tunnel crowd in the Big Apple at eight a.m.; the sidewalks equally spilled over with its citizens and tourists alike. It was enough to keep him occupied for the time being.

Sorenson rattled on about the Spanish conquistadores and how they discovered this area around 1499 or thereabouts, when they came upon the mouth of the Amazon River. But they didn't stay long and continued to forage into the northern region of Brazil. "Then, in 1669," he explained, "the Portuguese moved in and established their dominance by building a small fortress called the São José do Rio Negrinho."

"I assume to protect them from the horrid conquistadores, in case they returned?" Lance chimed in, feigning interest.

"Yeah, but it didn't keep out the missionaries that poured in from all religious sects to compete for souls. And as the village grew, it became known as Barra do Rio Negro. It wasn't until 1839 that Manaus became the official name for this settlement, after its indigenous river tribe, Manáos. And taking lessons from their rivals, the population expanded at a rapid pace. Give it to the Spaniards—they know how to propagate."

Lance noted a hint of a rare smile on Sorenson's face as he continued with the brief history lesson.

"Fast forward to the nineteenth century: the rubber boom dominated the region, and Manaus earned its nickname the 'Paris of the Tropics.'"

"All very fascinating." Lance tried to seem impressed, although he was rather indifferent. He had other more pressing items occupying his mind—like where the hell they were headed. "Swell gig you've got going."

Sorenson shot a look in his direction. "Not my gig. I'm here for one purpose only." The purpose was obvious.

"So—where are we going?"

The history lesson ended abruptly. Sorenson went mute and returned to form.

Any further attempt on Lance's part to pry out the purpose of this little side trip failed. Left in captivity, he stared out the window, viewing the traffic, until his thoughts drifted back to the last conversation he had had before leaving his office. The unknown caller warned him of the dangers, but shared little else, other than to follow Sorenson's directions without exception. One last snippet of information passed on, was that if he were successful it would change millions of lives for the better. The *if he were successful* bothered him the most.

"We're here," Sorenson uttered.

The Hummer swerved into an open gate and within seconds its engine shut down. In front of them was a sizable building made of rusted corrugated metal. Lance concluded, as he glimpsed the building along with the runway and wind sock, that the building was an airport hangar.

"Let's go." Sorenson reached around to grab a backpack from the rear seat and hopped out of the vehicle.

Lance followed.

Inside the hangar sat a twin-engine plane that looked like an old crop duster, except for the pontoons. As Lance got closer, he could see it was a two-crew AT-802 Fire Boss, used for both agriculture and firefighting. The configuration for the plane was for traditional take-off and landing on runways and waterways. What troubled Lance—it did not appear to be the latest model. At once, the George Bernard Shaw quotation rang in his head: "Both optimists and pessimists contribute to society. The optimist invents the aeroplane, the pessimist the parachute." *Thank God for pessimists*, he thought and then demanded, "Now, where the hell are we going?"

"Airão Velho."

"Where?"

"Novo Airão is a town of about fifteen to sixteen thousand inhabitants, founded by the Jesuits and settled by the Portuguese. It's one-hundred-forty-three miles upriver from here. On average, it's eighteen minutes of flying time. In this old bucket, closer to a half hour."

"But you said Airão Velho."

"It's the old ruins outside the town."

Lance was tiring of the question-by-question approach and opted to sit it out, or rather *pray it out* until they landed. Close to half an hour into the flight, he noticed they were heading toward a dense forest. Quickly, he began scouring the landscape, looking for a landing strip. Then, remembering the plane could set down on land or water, he prayed harder. It was a toss-up as to which one he preferred.

Sorenson thumbed his phone; at the same time, he appeared to begin his landing approach.

The texting while flying completely unnerved Lance. His prayers went straight into overdrive. And although he was not a practicing Catholic, he drummed up a few sins, and mouthed as many *Hail Marys* as he could before touchdown. On the tenth try to pay his penance, the plane bounced hard on the river surface and then jolted to the left, before jolting back to the right. Water sprayed outward from both sides.

Sorenson was nonchalant throughout it all as he spoke with someone on his phone. "We're here," he said, before ending the call.

Lance's prayers paid off, and the plane landed in one piece in the Rio Negro, just outside the remote village of Novo Airão. While Sorenson edged the plane toward the riverbank, Lance saw an odd-looking, dark-skinned man emerge from the brush. He was seated on a donkey, with another donkey in tow.

"Why are there only two donkeys?" Lance asked with unease.

"The man is a special doctor the local villagers call Macumba," Sorenson said, disregarding the question.

"You mean witch doctor? I came all this way to meet a witch doctor?" Lance wasn't sure if it was the jetlag, but he was certainly questioning his sanity.

"Go with him and he'll explain."

"What?!"

Sorenson ignored Lance's flareup and handed him a mosquito hat with a net mesh. "Here, you'll need this—and you have one hour; then I'm taking off. Now, c'mon get out."

With grave reservations, Lance grabbed the hat, checked his watch, and then gingerly stepped out of the plane and onto the pontoon. He edged himself toward the riverbank using caution, holding onto the plane's strut with a tight grip. The whole time he imagined swamp creatures circling in for the kill. And even though he knew there are no alligators in the Amazon, he knew of something as frightening called a black caiman. Lance kept a close eye until he stepped on solid ground.

After a few quick pleasantries in broken Portuguese, Lance awkwardly mounted the donkey, while the Macumba maintained the tangled rope around the poor creature's neck. In lockstep they lumbered into the dense forest that Lance had spotted from the sky. The heat appeared to dissipate as they moved under the roof of fauna, only to be replaced by a cold, clammy feeling. Lance felt every fabric fiber glued to his skin. He checked his watch again, as he rocked himself back and forth in a subconscious effort to urge the donkey to move faster. With great relief, the Macumba stopped at last and dismounted. Lance followed suit as inelegantly as he had climbed on. Without realizing he was standing in an ancient ruin, he noted the half-structured, stone buildings scattered about, covered by an overgrown jungle.

"Where are we?" he asked, impelled by the eerie graveyard feel.

"This is the place of our most ancient pharmacy, and I am the oldest ethnopharmacologist in the Amazon. My father, the greatest of Macumbas, brought me here as a mere child, over a hundred years ago."

"Excuse me, but how old are you?"

"I believe around one-hundred-sixteen years old." The Macumba waved his arms through the air to dismiss a trivial point and then stated with great pride, "You're surrounded by cures that treat all diseases."

"What diseases?"

"All," the Macumba repeated.

Lance's expression questioned his response, but the witch doctor piqued his curiosity.

"We Macumbas understand the medicinal uses of the various plants and use them in miraculous ways. Each one of us have our own specialty, our own combination of plants and species we harvest from this forest. We do not share our secrets with the outside world, but our way of life is being challenged."

"Challenged, how?"

"More researchers arrive in Novo Airão, desperate to understand our therapeutic uses. Their hearts may be present, but their footprints are destructive. So far, we have kept them from this sacred forest, but each year it becomes more difficult. Look around. There are over a hundred species of plants and over fifty animals we use, many of which can only be found here—in this ancient ground. Do you understand our hesitancy to share our ways?"

"Yes," Lance replied. He imagined what would become of this place if there were a foreign invasion, but the clock was ticking. "But that doesn't explain why I'm here."

"Stay. I will return."

The Macumba walked away and headed for one of the stone ruins. From Lance's vantage point it appeared to be well intact, compared to the other structures. At least the surrounding stones resembled walls. He checked his watch. By his estimation, he had twenty minutes left until the threatened takeoff. He became jittery. He was thankful the Macumba left the donkeys although he had no clue how to get out of the forest. Again, feeling trapped, he refocused on his sticky clothing and the thick air. Then, he heaved a heavy sigh of relief. The Macumba had returned.

Sorenson was hovering in the shade on the riverbank when he saw Lance walking toward him carrying a sizable black box. He must have missed the Macumba dropping off Lance while he was enjoying the end of his chain of cigs. "Let's move it!" he shouted.

As they flew back to Manaus, Sorenson noticed that Lance's eyes maintained a constant vigil over the cargo in his lap, seemingly afraid to let it out of his grasp. The rest of the flight lapsed in silence until they pulled into the old hangar.

"Now you know your mission." Sorenson stated.

Lance did not respond.

"Let's get you back to the hotel; you look exhausted." For the first time, Sorenson offered a sympathetic tone.

"What time tomorrow morning?" Lance asked.

"I'll pick you up at eight sharp. Your flight leaves for Monterrey at ten."

"Monterrey! Is this caper going to end soon?"

"When you arrive, you'll be instructed on where to cross at the Mexican border. A select group of beekeepers will be waiting for you to deliver the package. A few more hours after that it will be over."

Lance was tiring of the cloak and dagger mission and was more than ready to go home. But he had learned from the Macumba the vital importance of carrying out his assignment.

"See you at eight."

Chapter 2
The Annual Meeting

"Please, everyone; settle down."

The chairman gave the members an opportunity to take their seats before starting the meeting. Although the jam-packed room left many with standing room only, as the confab of beekeepers and honey producers from across the US was about to commence. The chairperson for the annual event was decided on a rotating basis, mostly a ceremonial gesture, although many of the beekeepers were also honey producers. Even some members belonged to both organizations. But this year, the official honor went to the President of the American Honey Producers Association.

"I call this meeting to order!" he called out, lowering the gavel onto the wooden podium several times with force.

The sound in the room within minutes drifted into silence.

"First, let me welcome our colleagues from the American Beekeeping Federation, along with all directors representing the State Delegates Assembly. It has been a tumultuous year for all of us with the wretched fires in the West and the record storms across our nation. Our winter was quite a doozy and may prove to be one of the worst for colony losses in a long time. But let's get cracking and see where we stand. Secretary Tillis, please review the latest stats for honey production."

"Thank you, Mr. Chairman. Per the US Department of Agriculture's latest statistics, they reported that honey production in 2016 was up three percent, totaling one-hundred-sixty-two-million pounds. The harvest of honey came from two-point-seven-eight-million colonies; up four percent since 2015. But honey prices in the U.S. were $207.05 per pound, down only slightly from 2015 at $208.03. We're still tallying this year's stats, but we've already received reports from various honey producers and pollinators alike, that the Thomas Fire in California added to massive losses. The heat alone destroyed the wax inside many of the frames from the hives and had an adverse effect on the bees, but the incineration of more than two thousands bee hives was devastating."

"Thank you, Secretary Tillis. And you're right about the Thomas Fire. Let's not forget the other fires that scourged California this year. The damage will be untold, including the thousands of acres of sage, buckwheat and other plants that burned to the ground. The bees have lost a great deal of excellent forage that will takes years to regrow," the chairman lamented, as he thought about how close he had come to the fire line. "Now, Hal," he redirected, "I understand you want to bring us up to date on CCD."

Dr. Harold Johnson, was an oncologist by training, with a PhD in entomology. He was exceptional, if not overqualified, as the president of the American Beekeeping Federation. "Yes, thank you, Mr. Chairman. I'm sorry to say, like Secretary Tillis's report, mine is also bittersweet." Hal turned to face the membership. "Most of us here have unfortunately experienced the destructive Colony Collapse Disorder when many of our worker bees disappear leaving the queen and the young behind. It's had a grave effect on our industry. We are, however, making some headway in staving off the honey bee's invasive pests: the varroa mite and tracheal mites, along with other diseases. But the greatest threat to our bees is exposure to certain pesticides. In fact, it has never been more difficult to keep our bees alive and healthy than it is today."

One delegate shouted out, "You forgot to mention the stress factor imposed on the hives during transportation! That's a great contributor to CCD."

Hal was aware that there was disagreement among the membership when it came to the topic of transporting the bees to provide pollination services. He readied himself. "Bees have been moved all over the country for many decades without major health issues. Bees have been shipped from Maine all the way to California for almond pollination for years. They arrive healthy and ready to get to work. With all due respect, I disagree with the transportation theory that's always bantered about when discussing CCD. But whatever the cause, we all have agreed that hives without worker bees would devastate the industry." Hal did not necessarily want to prolong the discussion because he was aware the "beemageddon" hysteria was still an active debate among the members. Once again, he prepared for opposition as he continued.

"Granted, we lost forty-four percent of our honey bee colonies between April 2015 and April 2016. However, between January and March of this year our loss is less than twenty-seven percent compared to the same quarter last year. In the last five years, we've lost one-point-two-billion dollars in the cost of bees. Not all can be contributed to CCD, given our typical loss runs about thirty percent."

A hand shot up in the air. This time the delegate waited to be acknowledged.

"The chairman recognizes the gentleman from the Sunshine State of Florida."

"Thank you, Mr. Chairman." The Floridian turned and faced Hal. "It should not be overlooked that with the combined efforts of the Honey Bee Health Coalition and the Pollinator Health Task Force, co-chaired by the USDA and the EPA, we've made great strides."

"In my humble opinion," Hal responded, "their positive impact on honey bee health across the nation has been minimal. Since CCD hit us back in 2006, there has been no discernible downtrend in the number of honey bee colonies. In fact, we're up sixteen percent. We didn't need the government mumbo-jumbo to show us how to split our healthy colonies and create multiple hives. Besides, they like to use us as an excuse to spend money."

The membership knew where Hal was heading and allowed him to vent.

"Remember that 'Pollinator Health Task Force,' the one the *Apology Tour* administration concocted to promote the 'the health of honey bees and other pollinators,' the one that asked for eighty-two-million in taxpayer dollars to reduce the honey bee colony loss and enhance seven million acres of land for pollinators? They also threw in some money to increase the population of the monarch butterfly. Just what we needed."

The discussion edged up a few notches on the thermometer when another colleague from Florida stood up to add his two cents. "CCD is an exaggeration by the environmentalists wanting to push their agenda against global warming, genetically modified organisms, and pesticides, to name a few. It's their perspective I have a problem with, and it deserves more of our attention—and whether we need to spend taxpayer dollars for more important environmental concerns. With our seven-hundred-million-dollar industry, our honey bees are just fine."

Hal took the floor back. "Excuse me, but our bees are not just fine! I mentioned earlier that pesticides are a major concern. And in this regard the environmentalists are finally fighting on the right side of the fence."

The delegate countered, "Shawn Regen from PERC, the Property and Environment Research Center, has been writing articulately about this subject for years. Perhaps he put the scary stories about CCD in perspective, when he quoted the words of Hannah Nordhaus, author of *The Beekeeper's Lament.* She said the reports 'should serve as a cautionary tale to environmental journalists eager to write the next blockbuster story of environmental decline.'"

Loud applause resonated in the room until the chairman pounded his gavel calling for order and returning the floor to Hal.

To tamp down the rhetoric, Hal allowed, "Perhaps, their focus is somewhat misguided." It worked. Those riled up, appeared to calm down. He continued. "We know there's no one culprit and we've weathered the storms in the past. But due to the hard work and dedication of the nation's beekeepers, the honey bee colony numbers have annually rebounded from the extraordinary losses we've suffered. However, being resilient should not preclude us from being proactive. Let's talk about what can be done."

"You have my attention. Tell us—what can be done?" That time the Florida delegate appeared to rest his case.

"More emphasis on planting flowers and trees that can survive the winter is a start. We all recognize that the lack of nectar available to feed the hives continues to be a crucial problem in certain geographic areas. Everyone should resist cutting Ivy plants, specifically in the genus *Hedera*, such as the Helix or Hibernica. These mature ivies with oval leaves bloom flowers in the fall and are an ideal source of food, producing high-quality nectar with forty-nine percent sugar. Also, planting a variety of flowering bulbs can provide a constant source of food with blooms ranging from early spring to late fall. Look!" Hal emphasized, "bee pollination contributes to nearly twenty billion dollars in US food production. It wouldn't hurt for every citizen to be educated as to the importance of bees to our economy!"

At that point, Hal was preaching to the choir. They were proud of their industry, both the pollinators and the honeymakers. They wanted everyone to understand their vital importance to the food chain.

Another hand in the air vied for attention.

"I recognize the gentleman from the great state of North Dakota," said the chairman.

"No one has brought up the Food and Drug Administration's latest intrusion. Effective January first of this year, we can no longer buy bee antibiotics, such as oxytetracycline, tylosin, or lincomycin over the counter, which we desperately need to maintain the health of our bees. Now, we must go to a veterinarian to get a prescription," the delegate huffed. "What the hell does a vet know about bees?"

"They're concerned with antibiotic resistance," offered one defender.

"As if we don't know how to diagnose and treat the problem," the gentleman from North Dakota refuted. "First, 'resistance' is an activist's code word for wanting to place controls. Perhaps, however, it's more about Big PhRMA wanting to get their hands into our billion-dollar industry. Once the over-the-counter antibiotic for a bee became a prescription drug—the price went up. The FDA also made the process extremely problematic and time-consuming for the vet."

"Only one-fourth of US beekeepers find it necessary to use the antibiotic," the defender countered.

"Might I remind you, during the summer months, North Dakota is by far the most densely populated honey bee state in the nation with more than five-hundred-thousand colonies. Pay attention! Without easy access to the antibiotic we run the risk of the American Foulbrood returning." The North Dakotan sent a chill through the chamber by mentioning the easily transmittable disease that kills bees with millions of infectious spores. "And let's not forget the FDA's been messin' with our honey." The point was well taken. The defender took his seat.

It was no secret that yet another spat with the FDA had been brewing. It had to do with the push to include 'added sugars' as a labeling requirement. The American Beekeeping Federation had weighed in publicly, stating that, "it would be much more logical and prudent if the FDA would consider listing the naturally occurring sugar content of 100% pure honey as 'Total Sugars' and not 'Added Sugars'."

Another hand shot up.

"I recognize the delegate from the state of Georgia."

"This label nonsense is misleading at best," he retorted. "What our labels should say is that honey contains forty percent *natural* fructose, and thirty percent *natural* glucose. Of course, that's an average percentage depending on the floral source of the nectar, but it's still a simple *natural* sugar and less than a complex sugar. You'll find that to be an average of ten to twenty percent higher, in both fructose and glucose. Don't forget honey also has the added benefits of propolis and minerals, including magnesium and potassium. And sugar not possessing those natural additives, puts it way higher on the glycemic index than our natural honey."

"It's a damn shame," interjected another man from the Peach State, not waiting to be recognized. "Honey should be marketed as a food, not a sugar. It also contains antioxidants and antimicrobial compounds, none of which sugar can claim to have. Simply put, honey supports the body's health—sugar does not. And as Secretary

Tillis reported, we produced over one-hundred-sixty-two-million pounds of honey in 2016. We're a multi-billion-dollar industry and the government continues to subsidize the US sugar industry, costing taxpayers nearly three billion dollars a year. Can't they do the math?! For certain they don't know their science."

Hal jumped back in. "Thankfully, the FDA has put that nonsense on the back burner for now and are not actively pursuing the issue." Hal attempted to put that hot topic to bed, but it had been a thorn in the side of the membership for years.

The tinder had been lit and produced a firestorm of conversation. There was no stopping the other members from chiming in, some heatedly, some marginally calmer, but no one silent. It was clear that all members of the State Delegates Assembly had something to grumble about. After another hour and a half of discussion points and reported statistics, the broad picture had been painted. Questions were asked and answered.

"If there are no other points to be made, I ask that the Young Apiarists Project Committee stay behind once I adjourn." Then, per protocol, the chairman declared, "I call this meeting to be adjourned. Do I hear a second?"

"I second the motion!" called out one of the delegates.

The gavel dropped.

All in attendance not asked to stay behind dispersed. They were content to be left out of the YAP committee, with its mission to establish an internship to study CCD. They were also satisfied to be the benefactors of its findings, without having to put in the time.

Fifteen members of the YAP Committee remained seated in the chamber. Only they were privy to the project's real intent, including the fact that it was a ruse. The made-up name, with a seemingly transparent purpose, appeared to satisfy the membership and provided the necessary obfuscation. When the last of the members trailed out of the chamber, closing the door behind them, the president of the American Beekeeping Federation spoke to his captive audience.

"The package will arrive in the next seventy-two hours. Are all of you clear as to the next phase?" Hastily, Hal raised his index finger to his lips. "Show of hands only!" he requested, encouraging a minimum of conversation.

All hands rose.

"In three days, we convene at this location." Hal held up a stack of business cards. "Safe travels," he offered, as he waited for the members to approach.

Each member of the bogus committee stood up. One by one, they lined up to receive a handshake, along with a business card that provided essential instructions for their next meeting. Retreating at a hare's pace, they left the chamber and the building before speaking a word. Once safely outside, they paid their respects with warmer gestures before departing to their various home states.

Chapter 3

The Ears ofThe Consortium

The Consortium's elusive director, always shrouded in secrecy, relied on a middleman to maintain his arm's length from the muck. For the past several years, Senator Erog had proved to be a viable go-between, but his boundless treachery brought his life to an abrupt end. In retrospect, the director never should have selected one of the nation's legislators. They always had a skeleton hidden away in an undisclosed closet that made them more vulnerable. Never did the director expect Erog's skeleton to break loose, forcing him to take his own life. But the director's mouthpiece was like a planarian; a flatworm that can regrow its head. Soon after, the Consortium also reared a new head to replace Erog. This time around, the director reached beyond elected officials and selected one of the most gifted operators from the world of wheelers and dealers—Justin Slater was the perfect intermediary, a gifted lobbyist in the thick of Big PhRMA, who had everything to gain and would be essential to pushing their agenda forward.

In 2017, the Pharmaceutical Research and Manufacturers of America, along with the giant pharmaceutical companies, comprised an industry that spent $209,395,967, supporting 1403 lobbyists, with $57 million allocated for federal lobbying; $8 million alone was spent in the first quarter, up 35% from the year before. What makes them unique as an industry is that they outspend every other industry in both lobbying efforts and in advertising that saturates all realms of the media. Today, worldwide PhRMA drugs exceed a trillion dollars in sales. And over the years, billions of those dollars washed onto the shores of the Food and Drug Administration, only to be returned in an ebb and flow of profits from the government's Medicare and Medicaid drug plans to Big PhRMA. In 2015, taxpayers funded the FDA with $331.6 million, but seventy-one percent of the funding, totaling $791.1 million, was provided by the drug companies. Hardly what one would consider an independent agency. Some have concluded that the FDA is addicted to drug money.

This unholy alliance, in part orchestrated by the director, made it easy pickings for the Consortium to find lobbyists from Big PhRMA willing to get their hands dirty—if they thought it were for the right cause. Yes, Justin Slater was the ideal choice.

"What's going on?" the Director asked. "I saw an opinion piece in the *Wall Street Journal* the other day about positive breakthroughs in biotech."

"It was only a matter of time before gene therapy would come into its own," Slater replied. "As you read in the article, Spark Therapeutics is showing promising results with Luxturna in treating retinal dystrophy. Sangamo Therapeutics is another one getting close to being able to edit genes directly. The medical advances are booming in such a way that cell-based gene therapy will become the answer to treating persistent cancers and other diseases."

"How's the FDA reacting to these trials?"

"They appear to be picking up the pace since the president's man Gottlieb took over at the helm."

"While POTUS was whipping out his pen to repeal his predecessor's legacy, he could have helped us out by repealing the 2012 Safety and Innovation Act."

"You mean the one that allows the FDA to hand out priority-review vouchers to drug companies, which they can later redeem to have other drugs fast-tracked?"

"That's the one; the original intent designed for tropical diseases was later expanded to include research in rare pediatric diseases. Keep your eye on the situation. So far, the FDA has been left to operate without oversight, but Gottlieb wants more transparency, forcing the FDA to explain the delay or rejection process. We must make sure they don't lose their regulatory tradition and entitlements. We can't lose control over the FDA. Now, what did you find out concerning that other matter?" the Director asked in an altered voice.

"My source reported something about a package arriving within seventy-two hours."

"What package and where?"

"I don't know. After the meeting adjourned, which provided nothing beneficial other than their usual carping, the members of a committee called YAP were asked to stay behind. I suspect the committee was a phony because my source said they didn't discuss much of anything. Most of the time they were silent."

"What, were they using smoke signals?!" The director was losing patience.

"I don't know if they were using hand signals or writing things down, but they didn't talk much. Minutes later, they left."

"Brilliant! They know they're being bugged and are not taking any chances. Find another way, Slater. I don't care how. Just find out what's in that damn package!"

The American Beekeeping Federation always seemed embroiled in controversy with the FDA constantly breathing down their hives. Whether it had to do with drugging their bees or labeling their honey, it was time-consuming and costly. Worse yet, several members were under federal surveillance—one was an FDA whistleblower. These strange bedfellows caused the director to use any resource to uncover the connection. Unbeknownst to the Federation, they had become the bullseye on the Consortium's target.

Chapter 4

Bereave Not

Max, unable to sleep, curled up on the sofa and soaked up the silence. It left her feeling empty, shallow, removed from reality. She reflected on her life as though she were standing on the outside looking in. Faces of blame spun in her mind. Faces of those she had loved, those she had befriended, those she had trusted. Reality had betrayed her again. Death was everywhere. Max stared at the empty glass; Old Mr. Jim Beam was empty too—the bottle neither half-full nor half-empty—void of any usefulness.

"Snap out of it, Max! The bourbon is doing the thinking for you." She held her head tightly in her hands as though she could squeeze out the demons. Without warning, the phone rang, breaking the deafening silence. She noticed the name on the caller ID and the time; the clock hands were aimed at a few minutes past midnight. *Timing sucks, Allison.*

Allison was her best friend and schoolmate throughout college. For Max, Allison was the sister she never had. And even though their life's ambitions took off in different directions, the emotional bond held them tight. Allison trained as a flight attendant and headed for the wild blue yonder; Max trained for the CIA.

The phone rang continuously, with no sign of conceding.

"Dammit!"

"Hey, what's up?" Max asked, steadying her voice.

There was no immediate response. Then, in a barely audible murmur Allison said, "Jeff's dead."

"Oh, God!" Max gasped. "What happened?" The sobering question momentarily replaced her personal despair.

"They said a heart attack—but it seems farfetched and I don't believe them! Jeff had a heart like a raging bull. He took great care of himself." Allison rattled off in denial, sketching in the details, searching for words to make it untrue. Her initial response turned despair into disbelief.

Max focused on only one word. "Who's *they?*"

"What? Max! You have to find out what really happened!"

"Allison, calm down. Tell me what they said." Max tried to focus while the jackhammer in her head worked overtime.

"An official from the State Department. He arrived at the house a few hours ago. He said Jeff was found unconscious in a hotel room in a Godforsaken place in Brazil. Something like Manos, Manus. I don't know. They're flying his body home tonight. The plane arrives at nine." Allison delivered her words at a drumbeat pace and then became incredulous. "They want to conduct an autopsy! Max, cut him open!"

"Sweetie, it's standard protocol for any government official who dies on foreign soil. But why was Jeff in Brazil in the first place?"

"I have no clue. It sounds pathetic, but he never brought his work home. Once he stepped off the Hill and walked through the front door, he focused strictly on the kids. All I can tell you is he's on several Senate investigative committees. Perhaps the trip was related to one of them. He was like you—always playing amateur sleuth."

Hope she's not implying I'm playing, or worse, an amateur. Max brushed off the inference and asked, "Has Jeff been on any other trips in recent weeks?"

"He's been in Washington for the last two weeks, which is highly unusual. Before that, he was in New Mexico for one night." Allison sounded peeved.

Max picked up on her uncharacteristic tone. "What's going on?"

"The life of a senator! Jeff traveled at least once a week. Convenient overnighters. Hmph," she sniffed.

The lightbulb lit up. "Allison, you're not serious? You don't believe Jeff was having an affair?"

"I honestly don't know what to believe. His behavior has been awkward for the past several months. When I tried to speak with him, he said it was business and blew it off. After a while, I stopped asking—then we dropped the subject."

"Sweetie, I'm sorry. But I'm sure there's an explanation. Jeff loved you and the kids. He'd do nothing to jeopardize your marriage."

"Max, you're not the one that lived with him. Leave it alone. Why do you want to know about his travels anyway?"

"I'm just trying to grab on to something."

"It's pointless now." She paused. "Odd... I always worried the next election might send us packing. I never considered that I'd have to pack alone. I'm a senator's wife. What the hell am I supposed to do now?!"

"You do nothing. Take time to grieve; be with the kids. You'll have plenty of time to figure things out later. In the meantime, I'm here for you. All you need to do is ask."

Sounding devoid of emotion, Allison asked, "Can you drive me to the airport tonight? I'll need a friendly body to hold on to." In an instant, it hit her. She was going to meet her husband coming back from a trip. Something she had done hundreds of times. This time she would greet him at the cargo hold in a coffin. The moment arrived. She could hold back no longer. Allison broke down and wept.

Max gave her a few moments and when the sobs subsided, she agreed. "I'll pick you up at eight."

When the line went dead, Max sat back, recalling another more pleasant phone conversation years ago, almost as if it were yesterday. Allison had returned from Paris where she had met the man of her dreams; it was love at first sight with the first-class passenger seated in 2A. For six hours, she literally wined and dined him. Max managed a chuckle, remembering Allison's complaint. "Only problem is, Max, he's a United States Senator and a Republican!" But in a year's time, Allison adjusted and became Mrs. Jeffrey Lance. For fifteen years, she lived as a senator's wife inside the Beltway. *Now, what will she do indeed?*

Max made an emergency visit to the kitchen and returned to the sofa holding a half-full glass. She opted to leave temptation and the fresh bottle of bourbon behind on the counter. "Here's to you, buddy!" she saluted and took a sip of the oaky brew. As it warmed her throat, another face flashed before her. He was the one person who, through an odd set of circumstances, she came to rely upon; the one person who wanted nothing from her in return. She hit the *speed dial* button and waited for the phone to complete the dialing.

"Haaaay, what are you up to?"

"Princess, it's one-thirty in the morning. What do you think I'm up to?"

"Sorrrry, Sam. I couldn't sleeeep."

"You okay? You don't sound like yourself."

Max mustered her strength and then forced out the words. "Jeff Lance is dead."

"The senator?"

"Yeees, he had a goddamn heart attack in Brazil."

"I'm sorry. Were you close?"

"Whendoesdeathstop?" Max slurred.

"Honey, you're not making any sense."

Max took another sip from her glass. Ironically, it had a sobering effect. Anger suddenly replaced despair. "Death! I'm talking about death! Jax died of a fucking aneurysm! Noble tried to kill me and ended up dead himself. You, near death, ended up in the hospital with two shots to the chest. And I left Stanton for dead. All this carnage because of me!"

"Stop it! Daniel is responsible, not you!"

"Daniel is my brother—my flesh and blood—and he's still out there!"

Sam remained silent, assessing her level of anguish.

"Sam. Sam, did you hear me?!"

"I hear you. But there's no reason for Daniel to come after you. Max—look, it's over! We're alive! You're the heroine—and one tough lady at that. You took down Erog. You exposed their hoax. You crippled the Consortium."

A sudden image of her holding the gun to Erog's temple, caused a wave of nausea and the realization—of how far she might have gone. *Thank God, he opted for cyanide,* she thought.

Her venting about past events concerned Sam. He hoped it was just her favorite drink talking. "Hey, princess, what's with the drama?"

"It hurts so damn much. I miss Noble! I loved him and trusted him!"

"That bastard! He betrayed your trust and was about to kill you! Frankly, I'm glad he's dead!"

"He betrayed himself," she murmured. Then with more fury, she cried, "That damn Consortium! How could they coerce him into believing their sick version of utopia?!" Max's anger funneled through her slurred speech.

"To control the earth's resources. To control the population. All for the betterment of mankind. It's all bullshit! It's so bloody unfair!" she lamented.

Sam caught the despair in her voice. He toned down his own rhetoric and tried to assure her. "I heard someone say once that, 'unfair is a term created by the weak because they can't defeat the strong.' That's not you, princess. Now, go pour yourself another stiff drink, tie one on, and then go get some sleep."

Suddenly, a friendly wave of exhaustion hit her. She did not fight it and agreed. "Good night, Sam."

Max hung up the phone and took another sip as she reflected on the time Sam had first called her "princess." It was on that horrible night when her father was killed. Sam, code name Casper, was the man with the piercing gray eyes, who crouched down, picked her up out of a pool of her father's blood, and carried her away to safety. At the time, Sam was carrying out a favor for his friend, Senator Sherman Spark. Twenty-five years later, under unusual conditions, Sam was called to do another favor at the behest of his friend—to save Max's life and a scientist's in the process. And they were the only two men in the world who knew her as Claudia Irving.

Chapter 5
The Beekeeper's Tour

"Mornin'. My name is Ollie Prince, and I'm the proprietor of this here Clovis Hill Apiary. I welcome y'all and commend you in your interest in maybe one day becomin' an apiarist. The bees need you! Follow me, and I'll explain why."

The high-school students sauntered behind Prince as he walked through the warehouse, inside of the apiary. Eyes darted about, but all ears tuned in with great interest, as he provided more details about the beekeeping business.

"As bee breedin' companies go, we're rather a li'l bidness, with only fifty hives housing a million bees. By comparison, the largest beekeeper in the US is the Adee Honey Farms, headquartered in South Dakota, with operations in California, Mississippi, and Texas. They've over ninety-two thousand hives; with bout forty thousand bees per hive. That's a dang woppin' three-point-five billion bees. Can you imagine that many buzzers?" He smiled as he caught a few of his young students zoning out. "But mind y'all, no matter how many bees, we still must stick to strict controls, providin' the proper nutrition and negatin' diseases, thus allowin' us to propagate them colonies at a fast pace. I understand most of you are thinkin' bout summer internships in an apiary. Give me a show of hands?"

All hands shot up, but Prince suspected no one wanted to look like they were just skipping a day of school.

"You take lots of notes now, and y'all *bees* that much smarter," he chuckled.

The group laughed, picking up on his humor, as they followed him outside into the field. The temperature was frigid, causing them to bunch close together next to the hives, but they paid great attention and listened as Prince provided a wealth of information. Every so often, a brave bee would venture out of the hive, but only for a second to eliminate body waste. Mostly, they stayed tucked inside and waited for warmer days to arrive.

Prince began by identifying the varying levels of beekeepers. "There're backyard and sideliners, like mahself, who have lesser of a focus on the commercial bidness, but we are important in our own right." He informed them that there are about eighteen hundred established commercial beekeepers, but in total, beekeepers contribute to 2.6 million hives in the US. "The entire industry is not made up of just pollination services, as we call us beekeepers, but also the farmers and growers and the bee brokers. We're all vital parts to the supply chain." He emphasized that honey production, however, is only thirty percent of the US supply, with most of the honey being imported, so the bees' major focus has been on the food supply. "Here's a little interestin' fact. We caint produce over a hundred different crops commercially in the US, without some form of pollination. For sure, wind and animal pollination contribute. But one third of the crops rely on bees to do the deed. Imagine that: one third of our crops need our bees."

Prince noticed the students shuffling their feet as they huddled even closer together, so he sped up his delivery of information. He rattled off a list of specific crops, vital to the food supply, noting that besides fruit trees, berry bushes, and vegetables, the bees also pollinate seeds, such as alfalfa, clover, and dandelion. He then cited statistics from the American Beekeeping Federation. "For example, California has more than one million acres devoted to almond production and provides eighty percent of the almonds worldwide. Each acre depends on pollination. It takes one-point-eight million colonies to pollinate that many acres. This is the largest single honey-bee pollination event in the world. And our honey bees are the best at gettin' the job done!" His statement was definitive, exerting enormous pride. "Now, who can tell me when the pollination cycle begins?" Prince asked, attempting to bring the students into the conversation.

One, standing in front of the group, shot out the answer. "In the spring, of course."

Prince nodded his head. "Actually, it depends on where the honey flows. Our motto is 'follow the bloom.' For almonds, the bees will pollinate in February and March, while other crops along the East and West Coasts may take place in March or April. So, y'all see it's vital to get the bees to the crops. But we must take care," he cautioned, "when transporting the hives for pollination, especially during the hot season." Prince explained that often the truck drivers would have to stop and hose down the hives to keep them cool. "It was not without risk. Sometimes a queen will pop out of the hive for a breath of fresh air and wander into another hive, risking her life as an alien invader. It's a rare occurrence because our beekeepers and truck drivers know how to haul the bees safely with the lowest impact on the health of the bees. And that's why we have plentiful crops and will be producin' the surplus honey between June and October. From November to January we concentrate on providin' nutrition to our bees endin' the cycle— questions, anyone?"

"How's the honey produced?" asked the same student.

"It's one of the miracles of nature." Even Prince, after years of being a beekeeper, marveled at one of God's gifts to mankind. He took pride and explained the process in a measured tempo. "When the honey bee pollinates the plants, the bee is rewarded by the flower's nectar. The little buzzer extends its tongue to do the job. Not a tongue like yours or mine. It's got three parts that wrap around to form a tube, like drinkin' straw. Then this li'l pump like device in its head turns on and sucks up the sweet juices into its 'honey sac,' which is separate from its regular stomach. It's like a li'l storage container." He looked around at the group to make sure he had garnered their attention. "Listen here: when that bee fills its stomach plumb full, it returns to the hive with its precious load of nectar. Then it reverses the li'l pump in its head to empty the honey sac. Droplets leaving the bee's mouth are passed on to mouths of the hive bees..."

"Yah, like kissing!" uttered one student. Spontaneous laughter broke out among his classmates as embarrassment washed across the young lad's face.

Prince winked at the student making the *faux pas* and then waited a moment for the group to settle down. "As I was sayin', when the nectar is transferred, it produces an enzyme called invertase." Slowly, he described how the enzyme helps to break down the nectar into two simpler sugars: glucose and fructose, before the hive bees spread the nectar throughout the honeycomb. "Then their fun begins," he said. "They start flappin' their li'l wings to fan the liquid causin' any water in the nectar to evaporate, leaving a thick syrup coatin' the comb. They're smart little critters because this becomes their source of food durin' the winter months. Ain't it amazin' what one'll do to stay alive?"

"But if they eat the honey, then where does your honey come from?" another student asked, a bit confused.

"Surprisin' enough, most hives produce a surplus of honey. That's what's harvested by the beekeeper and then processed for consumption. Remember, I sed we only produce thirty percent, with most of our honey bein' imported."

"You haven't mentioned the birds and the bees, or should I say queens and drones," stated a brazen student standing up front and center. He had yet to contribute, but now he appeared ready to step to the fore.

"Why don't you share with the group what you know?" Prince smiled at his attempt to tamp down the young lad's bluster.

"Ahem."

The other students giggled softly as the precocious one cleared his throat. They thought it was an obvious stalling tactic to prepare his answer, but were willing to wait.

Once composed, the student looked head on at Prince. "The drone only exists to mate with the queen bee to produce little worker bees. The queen has the tough job of giving birth to tens of thousands of these worker bees. And because she can live in the hive for one year or so, she'll be getting it on with many drones. After all, her job is to replenish the supply of worker bees, who literally work until they die. Poor little ladies only last a few weeks."

"Hmm, well done. But what happens to the drone once he mates?" Prince goaded.

"Poor guy dies soon after the fun," he replied offhandedly.

Prince opted to continue the repartee. "And why?"

Without hesitation, the student responded, "Because he left his penis in the queen. Clearly, why would he want to live?!"

The audacious student had his classmates doubling over, with Prince laughing in unison.

"You're correct," he snickered, "and for that reason most queen breeders allow their queens to 'open mate' naturally in the air, with drones, which in most cases, are of a desired genetic stock. As these breeders flood their mating areas with drones from selected colonies, it helps to ensure the quality of their mated queens."

"Brilliant concept!" chimed in another brave soul.

Prince assumed he was not referring to the bees and so did the other students. "Okay, class. Y'all had your fun; now let's go back in where it's warm."

With the wind picking up, there was no resistance from any of the students. But once inside the toasty corridor, another student pointed to the door at the end of the hall. "What's in that room?" he asked nosily.

"Ah, just an old storeroom of empty containers." Prince appeared to vacillate, and then provided a fast retort. "Waitin' to be filled with delicious honey!" He turned and veered to his left, leading the students into another corridor. Unexpectedly, a vibration emanated from his pocket. Prince held up his hand to halt the group. "Excuse me a moment."

Moving off to the side, he answered the phone. "What you want, Miss Ellie? I'm still here with the students."

"There's a gentleman here to see you. He says he's from the Federation. He don't have an appointment. Just sed he needs a few minutes of your time."

Prince checked his watch and noted it was ten minutes to the hour, almost quitting time. "Give me ten."

"Sorry for the intrusion," he said, returning his attention to the group. "Well, by now y'all shudda had a glimpse of the life of a beekeeper. Given the late hour, I'd be set to entertain a few more questions?"

The students appeared restless and were likewise ready to stop for the day. They each replied, not with a question, but with a various assortment of thank-yous.

"It wuz my pleasure," Prince replied. "And good luck with y'all's studies," he added, before shaking the hands of each of the students as they filed out of the facility. When the last one departed, Prince saw a man heading in his direction. He assumed it was the man without an appointment.

"Mr. Prince, I have information I need to discuss with you. It will only take a few minutes of your time. May I step inside?"

"Please, but make it quick. It's been a long day, and I promised the missus I'd be home for supper."

"Not a problem. I'll promise to make it very quick."

Chapter 6

Services Rendered

Max's head worked its way out of the bourbon-induced fog with help from a mighty strong caffeine brew. Once ready to leap into the day, she wandered downstairs and into her office to check her messages. Disappointment set in; there were none. She needed a diversion. She needed to keep busy. "Perpetual motion" was her byword. And while she was itching to dig her teeth into the next juicy case, she hoped it would not be wayward wives and senatorial scandals. She noted the time on the clock. It was just edging toward that hour, the hour she expected to receive a morning call from Noble. And even though it had been barely two months since his death, it was a call she still anticipated. *Eerie*, she thought as the phone rang. It gave her a sudden chill until she saw the caller ID.

"Hey, doll, how's your day going?"

From the sound of his voice, the call appeared innocent, but she suspected he was checking up on her. Agent Jake Stanton, once her lover, now played the invaluable role of a dear friend—something she needed greatly. He promised not to push. She took him at his word.

"It's only eight o'clock. And so far, it sucks."

"What's wrong, Max?"

"Jeff Lance is dead."

"I caught a quick mention on the news, but no real details. What happened?"

In a slow and disbelieving tone, Max explained that his body had been found in a hotel room in Brazil, dead of an apparent heart attack. The State Department was flying his body back to Washington that evening. "Once the coroner conducts an autopsy, we'll know more."

"It's tragic. How's his wife taking it?"

"She's devastated. I'm driving her to the airport tonight to meet the plane—the one bringing back her husband's corpse." Max wanted to get off the subject; she had dwelled on it long enough. "What did you want to talk about?"

Stanton rattled on for several minutes with trivial talk because his real mission was to check in on her. But from the absence of any usual retort, it was obvious her mind had drifted off in another direction. He made no headway. "Earth to Max."

"Stanton, you know that omniscient gut of mine?"

"Yeah," he replied, afraid of the answer he was about to hear.

"Right now, it's telling me this may be my next case."

"You mean the senator? Wait a minute—you *already* suspect foul play? You said it was a heart attack."

"I said an *apparent* heart attack! But I'll wait to hear the coroner's findings."

"That's unlikely," he uttered.

"What?"

"How about dinner tomorrow night? You could use some cheering up."

"You know, Stanton—what I could really use is some help."

"I thought you were going to wait for the coroner?"

"This is a just prelim—dipping my toe in to see if it gets wet."

"Sure it is," he chuckled. "Spit it out. What do you want me to do?"

"Jeff had an aide named Stefanie. She's a real knockout, so you probably know her already."

"Nice, Max."

"Use your charm. Find out why Jeff was in Brazil? Allison said he had been traveling a lot, but if you can get Stefanie to give you a printout of his calendar—say, for this year—that would be great!"

"Hey, doll, hold on. There's no official investigation yet."

"For Christ's sake, you're the head of the president's Secret Service detail—make one up!"

"I know this hit you hard but calm down! Remember, I'm still on leave and have no official capacity."

"Sorry, Stanton, but this whole thing with Jeff's death is making me squirmy. C'mon, you still have access to the White House. Just pay her a visit, please."

He knew the senator was well respected and a close friend of Max. He also knew Max's instincts were usually spot on. But when she resorted to pleading, it was serious. He wondered himself: *Could the senator have been a victim of foul play?*

"Please!"

There's that word again. "Remember the knife just missed my heart, so I still have one." Stanton relented. "I'll see what I can find out." And with Max's hound dog scent, he thought it needed repeating, "Don't sniff around until I get back to you. We'll talk about it over dinner tomorrow. Deal?"

"Deal."

"I'll pick you up at eight sharp."

"Thanks, Stanton. You're the best." Max hung up the phone, basking in her triumph.

Chapter 7
A Stinging Revelation

The trip to and from the airport was somber. Max used every ounce of resolve to keep it together while trying to console Allison. Allison's refusal to let Max stay the night did not make it less painful, forcing her to go home to dwell on her own tragic loss. After a day that seemed endless, Max stirred restlessly during what remained of a night's sleep. But by morning, she rose to the fore, revved up her spirits, and spun into motion. She was determined to find out what happened to Senator Jeffrey Lance.

"Stanton will be furious, but what choice do I have?" she said aloud, as though seeking confirmation from any source. Disregarding any potential answer, she grabbed her phone.

"Hey, Doc, have you conducted the autopsy on Senator Lance yet?"

"Good to hear from you too, Max. Funny you should call; I wrapped it up a few hours ago."

"Pulling an all-nighter?"

"Comes with the job description. And this one was a real bugger."

"Care to share?"

"Max—are you officially on this case?" he asked, more than curious. Then he realized the absurdity of the question, given the person on the other end of the line. *What the heck*, he thought. "C'mon over and see for yourself."

"Give me an hour!" she blurted out and then hung up the phone before the coroner had time to reconsider.

The Carmel Car Service swerved through traffic and pulled up to the curb in front of the Washington, DC, Medical Examiner's Building in no time flat. Max hopped out of the car and moved as skillfully as the driver, making her way to the coroner's office next to the morgue. A place that had become all too familiar.

"Morning, Doc."

"Rough night?" he asked.

Max smirked. She had hastily thrown herself together and it must have been obvious that her shuteye had been limited. "Now, how did the senator die?" She was eager to know his findings.

"Well, as I said, this was a real bugger. From the condition of the blood vessels throughout the entire body, it suggests that he had an anaphylactic response, a traumatic allergic reaction. The blood vessels were unusually expanded, which caused the blood pressure to drop suddenly. An inadequate flow of blood to the body's organs can likely trigger a severe attack of this sort, including a heart attack."

"So, what's he allergic to?"

"I questioned the same thing. I ran a complete tox screen."

"And?" Max's impatience started to peek through her armor.

"A bee sting!"

"Excuse me, how do you die from a bee sting?"

"Max, I just explained. But this was not your average bee sting. In this case, it was an extremely high dose of apitoxin—you know, bee venom. Normally, a bee can inject point-one milligrams of venom, but the toxicology report showed the dose of apitoxin was two thousand times more poisonous. Sure, a normal sting could cause inflammation, but at this level anaphylaxis kicked into high gear."

"You're telling me that the senator died from a severe allergic reaction due to a bee on steroids?!"

"Look: a lethal dose of apitoxin is about eight to ten stings per pound of body weight. Our corpse is one hundred and forty pounds. He would have had to have been stung fourteen hundred times, injecting one hundred and forty milligrams. The toxicology report shows two hundred milligrams."

"Thanks for the math."

"Hold on. I sent a copy of the tox report to the Center for Disease Control. They got right back to me and reported that there were no known strains that powerful and ruled out an epidemic. They plugged the info into their computer database and said they'd notify me if they hear of any similar cases."

"Great! No epidemic. But that doesn't help."

"Max, here's the conundrum. I found no evidence of a stinger— anywhere on the body. You'd think if there were over a thousand stings, I'd find one. And most bees don't have the capacity to remove the stinger. It's literally ripped from their abdomen, often leaving part of that behind as well."

"So, if a bee stung the senator, there must be an injection site. Don't look where you think he might have been stung; look where it'd be less likely. Doc, it must be there. Search again!"

"Smart girl. Follow me."

Max flinched and took a deep breath as she walked with the coroner to the massive steel wall of drawers, the temporary holding pen for unfortunate souls.

The doctor noticed Max's discomfort. "So, what's your interest in this case?"

"Friend."

"Hey, wait a minute. You sure?"

"Slide it out." Max averted her eyes in the opposite direction.

The doctor slid the gurney from behind the steel door. Then, after one more deep breath, Max watched as the sheet peeled away from the face of a once-dear friend.

"Check this out." The coroner turned the head a tad to the left and held a magnifying glass over a tiny purplish dot—an injection site. "When I couldn't find the stinger, I resorted to shaving the body and looked again. Some son of a bitch injected this poor fella by placing the needle in a hair follicle. To do so, the killer would have had to knock him out first before meticulously injecting him."

The coroner scratched his head.

"What is it?"

"What had me puzzled was the slightly elevated dose of chloroform that appeared on tox report. But I blew it off because that level can usually be attributed to water, like a daily shower when the chloroform in the water naturally absorbs through the skin—now, it makes sense."

Max appeared stunned and did not comment.

"Are you listening?"

"Yes. You're telling me Jeff was murdered!"

"You want to sit down?"

Max waved her hand in the air and left the morgue, leaving the coroner to return the corpse inside the dark, cold drawer.

Chapter 8

Friendly Alliance

Stanton checked his watch and simultaneously hit the Uber button on his phone. On schedule, the car was waiting outside his condo. At last, he and Max were going to share an enjoyable dinner together, the one thing he had been anticipating throughout the day. He missed their intimacy; it had been a long time. But he was content to be the friend she relied upon, although he confessed to himself that one day he hoped it would lead to more. He also promised not to push, but then again, he thought, *tonight could be the night.*

"Have a good one," he said to the driver and stepped out of the car. As soon as both feet were planted on the ground, his phone vibrated. It was not a great start to the evening. It was a message from POTUS. He read the text. In that instant, the possibility of staying the night evaporated. He remained at the base of the steps leading up to Max's Victorian a while longer to delay the inevitable. But seeing the bronze plaque fastened on the brick outside her front door, emblazoned with the words,

Max Ford Private Investigations, made him smile. It was a gift from him.

Max heard the car pull up out front and assumed it was Stanton. When she opened the front door to greet him, he was still standing at the base of the stairs staring into his hand.

"Coming in?" she asked, in a less than cheerful mood.

"Hey, beautiful!" He slipped his phone into his pocket and headed up the stairs. But as he got closer, he could tell something was horribly wrong. "What's the matter?"

"Jeff Lance did not die of a heart attack—he was murdered."

From the look on Max's face, Stanton felt her pain. All he could do to console her was to hold her tightly in his arms. She did not resist. He embraced the moment and then suggested they go upstairs. Again, she did not oppose him. Still with his arm around her, they walked through the office reception area and upstairs to her apartment. Once seated on the sofa, he was careful to ask, "Tell me, what's going on?"

Max began to feel more at ease having Stanton seated next to her. In a quiescent manner, she filled him in on her visit to the coroner's office, steering away from the unnecessary gruesome details, maintaining her composure throughout.

He listened without interruption, and resisted razzing her for jumping on the case before he got back to her.

"So, you see—I was right to suspect something was amiss." Her voice was abnormally quiet and low.

"You generally are, my dear," he said, knowing full well there was no chance at that point that she would let it go. "You remind me of the Eleanor Roosevelt quote, when she said, 'A woman is like a tea bag; you never know how strong it is until it's in hot water.'"

"You're calling me a bag?" she teased. Her mood reverted to form, and she turned the questioning around. "Tell me what you found out." Her eagerness to learn of Jeff's travels was more than clear.

Stanton handed her an envelope. "Here's a printout of his appointment schedule. But I could only get the last six months. I hope this helps you find whatever it is you're looking for."

"You're amazing. Evidently, your charm worked. I won't ask what else it took."

"I didn't speak with Stefanie. I thought it best to keep a low profile until there's an official investigation."

"Then where did you get this?" She waved the envelope.

"Didn't they teach you in spy school never to disclose your sources?" Stanton winked. "If I tell you, then I'll have to kill you."

She shined a hint of a smile as she reviewed the list of appointments. "I guess I'll have my work cut out for me tomorrow."

"I know this is a futile attempt on my part, but can't you let the authorities handle the case? They'll be swooping in as soon as the coroner reports his findings."

"No, I have to follow through on this one."

"Does Allison know?"

"No, and I told the doc to hold off briefly until I break the news to her. I should be the one who tells her that her husband was murdered. But not until after the funeral. She needs to get past that first because this will hit her hard."

Stanton shook his head. "I thought in the PI biz that first you get the client and then you get the case."

"You sound like…" Max caught herself as a vision of Noble flashed in her mind. She reverted to topic. "But I have a client." A picture of Jeff lying supine on a cold, metal gurney quickly replaced her earlier image. "He just can't tell me what happened."

"I didn't know Jeff on a personal level, but I heard he was an honorable guy. His wife deserves to know the truth."

"Thank you for understanding."

"Just promise me you'll be careful out there. You have a magnetic touch for danger. Now, about that dinner?"

"Do you mind if we order in? I'm really not in the mood to go out."

"Sure, doll!" Stanton replied with great relief. Having dinner ordered in made it easier to call the night short. POTUS was expecting him in the Oval Office at ten o'clock.

"Sushi?" Max asked.

"Sounds great."

While Max left to order, Stanton remained seated on the sofa, contemplating what the president possibly needed to discuss so late at night. He was still on medical leave for another two months, so he suspected it was not work-related.

"Done!" she said as she walked back into the living room carrying two glasses of wine. Her mood had taken another turn for the better.

After a clink of their glasses and few more sips, Stanton mustered up the courage. "Hey Max, I'm gonna have to cut out early. The prez asked to meet later."

Max took a few seconds as her internal alarm sounded off in her head. "What does he know about that night—the night you were attacked?"

Stanton sensed a tad of paranoia in her question. "Only that I was trying to stop a break-in. And the burglar got away."

"That's all?"

"Max, I didn't realize at the time what you'd gotten yourself into, but I kept your name out of it. Don't sweat it. He probably wants to see how I'm doing. That's all!"

"Not sure if you were aware, but Noble had become the president's personal truth-seeker."

Where's this coming from? he thought, but allowed her to continue.

"He told me that in the current political climate, the president didn't know who to trust, whether it be the FBI, CIA, DEA, DOJ, or any other agency. POTUS needed eyes on the ground. At least that's what the president told Noble." She paused. "Maybe you'll become his next pair of eyes?" Her question was not without suspicion.

Stanton remained silent, trying to figure out what was spinning through her overactive mind. But it soon became of no import as Max flipped back into an aggrieved state. It was obvious Jeff's death had hit her hard. And not wanting to push his luck, he let it go. "Let's enjoy the time we have."

He set down his wine glass and reached over to hold her in his arms. For a second time, she did not resist. He happily enjoyed the moment until the doorbell rang. "You stay here. I'll go get the dinner," he offered.

Chapter 9

Spy To Spy

The sushi dinner was tempered by Max's disposition and the night was cut short by POTUS. But a surprise visit early the next morning found Max in an unpredictably pleasant mood. She was already busy at work in her office scouring Jeff's appointments, when Stanton reappeared.

"What's the matter—can't stay away?" she teased.

He smiled and handed her a package.

"What's this?" she asked, as she unwrapped her gift.

"I know how much you like croissants."

"No, I mean this," she said, shaking the flaky crust off the wrapping.

"A peace offering for having to leave early. It's Jeff's personal calendar. I found it hanging out in the cloud."

"Thanks!" Max said, seeming a bit surprised.

"Read nothing into it. I started thinking perhaps it wasn't Capitol business that got the senator killed. Lucky you, my computer hacking skills are like riding a bicycle." Stanton sniggered and soon realized it was out of place. And lucky for him, his quip went unnoticed.

Max was already studying the new list of appointments.

"All's forgiven?" he dared to ask.

"Nothing to forgive. What did POTUS want?"

"Nothing earth shattering. Only what I suspected. How am I doing? When was I coming back? Basically, I think he misses his jogging partner." Stanton attempted to make light of the conversation.

Max wondered whether it was all that innocent, but let it go for the time being. She put the paper down and reached for Stanton's hand, which surprised him. "Hey, sorry for being so bitchy last night. I just couldn't get Jeff off my mind."

"It's understandable, but remember you don't have to be Super Sleuth all the time. Something or someone got Jeff killed. Walk this one carefully."

"I will. And much appreciated." She pointed to the paper spotted with flakes of buttery pastry.

Catching the time, Stanton leaned in for a quick kiss on the cheek. "I really have to go."

"No problem. Thanks to you, I have work to do." Max walked him to the front door, where a car was waiting for him. Out of nowhere, another car pulled up to the curve. As Stanton's car pulled away, a lanky man with graying hair and piercing gray eyes stepped out of the vehicle.

"Casper, what the hell are you doing here?!" Max shouted.

The surprise visitor made his way up the steps as she remained standing outside her front door.

"Okay, so what gives?" she asked.

"You sounded a little lonely the other night. I thought you could use some company."

"I don't buy it."

"Clearly, I was mistaken." He grinned as he looked down the street. "The Secret Service agent was leaving your abode rather early this morning." The mischievous grin returned.

"Well, now that you're here, I can't leave you standing at the doorstep. C'mon in," she invited, blowing off his inference.

He set down his carry-on in the reception area and inspected the first floor of her office dwelling. "Nice. It shows off your decorating skills."

"Ha-ha, my decorator will be offended. Why are you really here?"

He walked over to her office and peeked in and then eyed the vacant office across the hall. "That's Jax's?" he asked.

Max realized ever since Jax's death, she had never gone back into his office. Everything remained undisturbed. She nodded.

"What do you say I give up my palm trees and sandy beaches for a little while—and hang out here? I'm sure you can find something to keep an old, crusty spy busy."

Who's the lonely one, she began to wonder, but admittedly, she was glad he was there. "I don't take on freeloaders. But if you're willing to help me work a case?" She hinted, flashing a huge smile that would put a Cheshire cat to shame.

"On one condition. Can the code name—call me Sam."

"I don't know what you're up to, *Sam*, but I could use help. Another pair of eyes to see what I might have missed. By the way, the pay's lousy. And where do you plan on staying?"

"I'll find a place." He shrugged his shoulders as he glanced toward his luggage.

"Okay, you can stay in the guest room. But remember what they say about guests and fish."

"I'll be out of here in three days. Let your agent man know the coast will be clear after that."

"There's nothing between Stanton and me; it's purely platonic. We're just good friends. And Sam—he knows nothing about Italy. Let's keep it that way."

"Sure thing, princess." He smiled as he thought, *mission accomplished*. "So, what case are we working on?"

"Jeff Lance."

Sam looked confused. "You said he died of a heart attack."

Max filled him in on the details of her meeting with the coroner and his findings.

"Bee venom?" Sam asked.

"It's murder, pure as honey, no matter the method. Now, go get yourself settled in, grab a cup of coffee, and meet me in my office."

Seated behind her desk, Max found it comforting to have Sam around. She never would admit to needing a partner, but what she missed most was the synergy. First Noble, sometimes Stanton, and then Jax. There was always someone she could rap about the cases with, to look for clues, and share in the danger and excitement when presented. Casper, the spy, certainly had the credentials, considered one of the CIA's best. But Sam, the civilian, brought something else to the party. He had been her protector since her childhood. *Sam would make a great partner, even though I suspect he's here for another reason.* She shook her head. It was no time to speculate.

Max returned her attention to the case, eyeing between both lists, trying to decide where to start. *Jeff's business appointments or work off his personal calendar?* she contemplated. Opting to start with his business calendar, she hoped to find something, anything, that would lead her to Brazil. At first glance, she noticed each of the appointments appeared to be coded, some marked with a "NO" and others with an "O". *That helps,* she thought, *if "O" stands for official and "NO" stands for non-official.* A slew of acronyms also dotted the pages, seeming to indicate a committee. "Here's one H-E-L-P. That's one of Jeff's committees." She knew it was the U.S. Senate Health, Education, Labor, and Pensions Committee, because she considered the acronym an oxymoron. Her meager knowledge of the committee's activities included the fact that it tackled a host of issues ranging from the rising cost of pharmaceuticals to the Food and Drug Administration's user fee agreements.

"Hey, princess, talking to yourself?" Sam teased as he appeared outside her office door.

"Bad habit. Have a seat. I'm going over Jeff's appointment calendar, trying to figure out why he was in Brazil."

"Dare I ask how you got that information so quickly, Carmen Sandiego?"

She cocked her head.

"Oh, agent man."

"What makes you say that?" Max smirked and before he had an opportunity to retort, asked, "Would you call the Seringal Hotel in Manaus, Brazil, and find out what they know? Arrival time, discovering the body, visitors—you know the drill. Check in with the local authorities as well."

"So, I take it, this is *officially* our new case?"

"Yes, but this one's pro bono." Max paused, expecting some guff.

"Okay. I'll go call Brazil." He stood, offered a full military salute, and left to go play detective.

Max still wondered what Sam's angle was. *Why is he really here?*

"Well, I might as well start at the top of the list," she mumbled, and looked at the appointments again. In a process of elimination, she crossed off what appeared to be strictly committee business and focused on those names marked with an "O." She assumed for the moment, if she was correct, it meant official business because she recognized most of the names as those inside the Beltway. One surprising name kept popping up. It was Justin Slater, the infamous lobbyist for Big PhRMA. *Hmm, I wonder what he and Jeff had going on?* Max thought.

When she skimmed the list of appointments with various jumbled letters that indicated committee work, she became dismayed at the realization of how elected officials spend a great deal of their time. But then as she moved further down the page, she noted that several entries appeared to be airline flight numbers and departure times. Oddly, many were coded with a "NO." Harking back to Allison's concern that Jeff was playing around, she decided to switch directions, hoping to dispute the marital allegation. What was clear, his aides booked all his flights, both business and personal. She looked at the final entry: Jeff's last flight. It read "AA324 / 1265 1:50 pm." Armed with the keyboard, she confirmed her suspicion. It was an American Airline flight to Manaus, Brazil, with a stop in Miami. He would have arrived at his destination that evening at 10:51, approximately nine hours later.

With only the last six months to work with, Max started in July with all non-official flights booked. American Airlines appeared to be Jeff's preferred airline, so she typed in the various flight codes directly on the airline's website. From the dates, Jeff traveled every week, but she concentrated on only those marked non-official, hoping Allison was wrong. The first trip appeared on July 5th, when he flew from Dulles International to San Francisco, with a stop in Los Angeles. On the twenty-sixth, he flew back to Los Angeles. On August 16th, he flew to Jackson, Mississippi. That was the only flight in August, even though Congress was in recess. But in September, he made two trips to Houston, Texas, but only one was marked non-official.

Max looked again at the list and skimmed the remaining months. It was plugged with "O's" and "NO's." *Sheesh, I need a different approach.* Her thought directed her attention to the last flight listed before Jeff left for Brazil. It was an entry from two weeks earlier which read: UA6018/BA456 3:05 pm. Her weary fingers continued to tap on the keyboard where she discovered he had flown to Clovis, New Mexico. It became obvious that most weeks, Jeff took a trip somewhere. Without knowing why or with whom, it led her nowhere. "Nothing connects to Brazil. I give up!" she voiced aloud, and thrust herself back into the chair frustrated, until she remembered Stanton's butter-soaked gift.

She grabbed Jeff's personal calendar and meticulously scanned the list of appointments. Many appeared to be for kid functions—a recital, soccer games, a night at the opera, and a few marked "date nights." All of a sudden, Max's heart ached as she tried to imagine Allison coping with such an ordeal. *Argh, I feel like a voyeur.* The troubling notion caused her to cross off anything that smacked of family affairs and refocused on the remaining entries, attempting to pair them up with the flights. It was becoming clear that Jeff's aides booked the flights, but were not privy to their purpose. *It's time to test out my theory,* she concluded and began to match the flights with the names written down on the same day. Jeff's personal calendar listed the name Rowen on July 5th, Boroch on July 26th and Blaylock on August 16th. Both flights in September to Houston corresponded with the name Burzynski. "Aha! Maybe now I'm getting somewhere," she said aloud.

Max did a Google search by typing in "rowen san francisco" and hit the *Enter* key. *Okay, the first four listed have to do with condos. I doubt Jeff was looking for an apartment.* The next one on the list was for a Dr. Robert Rowen, but his office was located in Santa

Rosa. *Not too far away from San Francisco. Could it be the same guy?* Max sensed she was closing in on a clue. She clicked on the website for information and read directly from the screen. "So, the good doctor is affectionately known as 'The Father of Medical Freedom for pioneering the nation's first law protecting alternative medicine in 1990 in Alaska.'" She was totally bumfuzzled. "Okay, Jeff what did you have going with this guy?"

Max's juices were flowing, so in the same fashion, she typed "boroch los angeles" and at once, the photo of Ann Boroch, with the caption: *Candida Healing and Multiple Sclerosis Expert,* appeared on the screen. She noted that Boroch was also a naturopath. "Bingo! This moves the ball forward." Hurriedly she typed "blaylock jackson mississippi" and again punched the *Enter* key. "Russell L Blaylock; another physician promoting alternative health." At that point she was becoming antsy. With only two more to go, she crossed her fingers on one hand and typed "burzynski houston" with the other hand. "Jackpot!" She discovered that Dr. Burzynski ran a clinic specializing in advanced alternative cancer treatment in Houston. Jeff had met with him twice, but one visit was marked personal. She sat back for a moment to contemplate. *Hmm, there appears to be a connection between the doctors, but what's the connection between them and Jeff?* For that answer, she would need more time and more resources. But she still had one more name to check out.

Max was curious why Jeff would fly to Clovis, New Mexico, on non-official business, two weeks before going to Brazil. She scanned the appointments, working her way down to December. A name almost leapt off the paper. The name was Clovis Hill. "Ah ha, like in Clovis, New Mexico." *Perhaps it's a company, not a person.* By that point her brainwaves were operating somewhere between Beta and Gamma. She double-checked the dates; they coincided. Reinvigorated, she tapped the keyboard until she pulled up the website for Clovis Hill Apiary in Texico, New Mexico, located only a few miles from Clovis. "Apiary—as in bees. What the hell's going on?!" She grabbed the phone and dialed the number for the Clovis Hill Apiary.

Max bolted into Sam's office and plunked herself in the chair across from him.

"What's wrong with you? You look like you just saw a poltergeist."

"Funny coming from a guy with the code name Casper." She flashed a full set of enamels before getting back on point. "This is serious. Two weeks before Jeff flew to Brazil he took a trip to Clovis, New Mexico—to an apiary. I called the company, and the number is disconnected."

"You're telling me the senator was hanging out with a bunch of bees and then goes to Brazil, four thousand miles away, and gets killed with bee venom."

"As unbelievable as it sounds, yes. There's got to be a connection."

"Well, I have information for you too. Listen to this. I spoke with the desk clerk at the Seringal Hotel, who was on duty that night. He said Jeff arrived shortly before midnight. He checked into his room and never left until morning."

"Was anyone with him?"

"The clerk said no; he checked in alone. But around eleven thirty the next morning, when he entered the lobby, he was greeted by a man who he appeared not to know."

"Why did the clerk think the man was a stranger?"

"According to him, the guy had been waiting in the lobby for a while. When Jeff arrived, the desk clerk noticed the guy looking back and forth from Jeff to his phone. The clerk assumed the man was checking for a photo ID."

"What happened next?"

"They exchanged words. Then Jeff returned to the front desk, retrieved his key and left for his room. Five minutes later, he reappeared, dressed more casually, and then departed with the stranger. Again, according to the desk clerk, Jeff returned that evening around six o'clock unescorted. He requested a morning wake-up call for six thirty and then left for his room. That's a wrap!"

"Did you get a description of the stranger?"

"My dear, I'm not that rusty. He was about six feet, two inches tall with aging blond hair and blue eyes. The desk clerk believed he might be Scandinavian, possibly Norwegian based on his height."

"Did Jeff have any visitors when he returned that night?"

"The clerk saw no one arrive other than hotel guests, until he ended his shift at midnight."

Max paused somewhat before launching the next question. "How was the body discovered?"

"A housekeeper. The manager called the local authorities. The moment they arrived they asked for a copy of Jeff's passport and discovered he was a U.S. citizen. It was the police chief who called the American Consulate and sealed off the room until a representative arrived."

Max sensed there was more to the story. His delivery was too cut and dried. "Anything else?"

Sam inhaled.

Max braced herself.

"The senator was found in a compromising position, showing he was not alone. His clothes were strewn about and there were two wine glasses, half consumed."

"So, the killer made it look like he had a heart attack during a love fest!"

"Perhaps," Sam allowed half-heartedly.

"What! You buy it?"

"Don't close off any possibility at this point."

"Any forensics?" Max groaned.

"That question we'll have to ask the State Department."

"It still doesn't tell us why he was in Brazil in the first place."

"This is all preliminary. How's it going with the appointment calendars?"

"It's not. Jeff met with the usual suspects and flew to various cities crisscrossing the country. But something seems out of place. First, it's the numerous appointments he had with Slater."

"Slater, the influence peddler for Big PhRMA? I've heard about him."

"Yeah, he makes 'black ops' seem like Sunday school. Slater knows no bounds and his tactics are less than conventional. But what's odd, is that Jeff was on several committees: one investigating Big PhRMA and another to regulate FDA fees."

"It's more likely that he was exerting pressure, rather than influence," Sam asserted.

"Possibly, but there's more weird stuff happening. In July and August, Jeff visited various doctors around the country that specialized in alternative medicine. But to be honest, I can't be sure about any of the doctors. There are only names and dates. That's where you come in, my friend."

Sam did not like her tone and braced himself. "Lay it on me."

"There's no way I can decipher whether the scheduled appointments were in-house or simply phone calls. And there is no way to figure out who he was flying off to see. I've only perused two months' worth. Now, I need your wizardry. I need Jeff's phone records—business and cell phone calls for the last six months so I can cross-reference them with his appointment calendars."

"I can see you're going to enjoy using and abusing me."

"Being an ex-spy comes with advantages."

"Your spy skills aren't so shabby."

"I can't risk my license. You took this gig; do some good."

"I'll see what I can do." Sam smiled. He was enjoying the repartee so long as Max did not catch on to his real purpose for his impromptu visit.

"Sam, out with it. Why are you here? You're a field agent—and you settle for a desk job."

What is she, psychic? Be careful, old boy; remember who you're talking to, he warned himself. "Hey, Max, these old bones have lost their luster for any undercover stuff. Spy-lite fits me fine. And you ain't too bad to look at either, boss. In all candor, I've enjoyed getting to know you. And relieved that you've learned the truth about your past. Don't over-analyze, princess. And try not to piss off any assassins this time around."

"I'll do my best." *I only hope Daniel will stay away. And I suspect that's what prompted Sam's appearing act.* She erased the thought for the moment. "Incidentally, I booked a flight to Clovis, New Mexico. I'm leaving after the funeral."

Chapter 10

The Numbers Game

Max was liking her new partner for many unexpected reasons. And given the short time they had worked together, it was humming along surprisingly well, almost as though they had worked together for years. Perhaps the revelation that Sam had been a part of her life behind the scenes made their new partnership seem natural. The fact that Sam aced his first assignment and delivered the goods was a great start.

Now with her antenna fully operational and armed with the list of Jeff's cell phone calls, Max could match the phone numbers that coincided with specific travel dates. She reasoned that if the senator's aides only knew about his non-official travels, but were not privy to their purpose, the calls made from his personal phone may be more telling. To simplify the process, she crossed off his home phone number, Allison's cell-phone number, and for now, any local numbers. After reexamining the list, she took a brief pause. Then she readied herself and dialed the call placed on July 2nd, only three days before Jeff traveled to San Francisco. The telephone number began with a 707 area code, located somewhere in Santa Rosa, California.

"Dr. Rowen's and Dr. Su's office. May I help you?" asked the perky female on the other end of the line.

Jackpot! "Yes, could you please tell me the doctors' specialty?"

"The doctors specialize in alternative and integrative medicine. Would you like to schedule an appointment?"

"Not now. Thank you." Max ended the call and reviewed her notes. She had concluded accurately that Dr. Rowen was the same doctor who Jeff flew to San Francisco to visit. *But why?* she pondered. After additional sleuthing, she learned Dr. Rowen and his wife, Dr. Su, offered a wide variety of nutritional therapies, along with specializing in oxidative medicine. They relied on both Eastern and Western medicine. What caught Max's attention was their use of ozone therapy and their claim it cured Ebola. She scoured the Net and happened on an FDA Federal Regulation. She read the specific section Titled 21, Volume 8, Section 801.415 (a) that stated:

Ozone is a toxic gas with no known useful medical application in specific, adjunctive, or preventive therapy. In order for ozone to be effective as a germicide, it must be present in a concentration far greater than that which can be safely tolerated by man and animals.

"What a surprise! The FDA disagrees." Further reading showed that in 2010, the FDA seized dozens of ozone generators sold for treating cancer, AIDS, and hepatitis. She learned that regulations varied from state to state, but according to the California Naturopathic Doctors Act they forbad the use of any gas.

"So, how do Rowen and Su evade the regulation? More importantly, what was Jeff's interest in these doctors?" It was a head-scratcher for sure, but Max deemed it was time to move along.

She skimmed over the long list of telephone numbers remaining, looking for any area codes for Los Angeles, Jackson, Mississippi, and Houston. *Jeff traveled to those cities. But to see whom?* she questioned. Max started the dial-a-thon and encountered a few misses, but then the next few calls became a series of bizarre hits.

The only number listed for Los Angeles rang nonstop: no answering machine, no disconnect. Frustrated, she decided to google "boroch los angeles" for a second time and delved deeper. *Oh my God!* Beyond the search listing she had read on her first try were various online health newsletters reporting that Ann Boroch hanged herself in her garage on August 1st. *This is rather disturbing, yet gripping,* she pondered. Then she stumbled on other news sources that reported detectives within the LA Police Department believed it was a professional hit, saying the crime scene was too perfect to be true. The only official source Max could retrieve was from the LA County Coroner's Office. It was the case detail for number 217-05693: Name Tami Boroch, Age 51, Cause of death: hanging. *This is so unbelievable. How could I have missed it?*

Max kicked herself. She had a peripheral knowledge from her first search that Boroch was a naturopath, researcher, and award-winning author of books on health and wellness—all information retrieved from her website. But further research, the second time around, revealed Boroch had healed herself of multiple sclerosis and had been symptom-free for twenty-three years. *Whoa! This is strange.* Boroch posted a blog titled, "Vegan Sunburgers for your Meatless Monday" two days before she reportedly hanged herself. *Not something you'd expect from a suicide-bound person. What's even more troubling is that no one had yet taken down the website.*

Max sat back and stared at the photo of the beautiful and talented naturopath. She tried to contemplate how bad it would have to be for you to want to take your own life—especially, in Boroch's case, someone who had overcome a life-threatening disease, and appeared to have a burgeoning career. All of a sudden, another site caught her eye. It was *YourNewsWire.com.* It noted that Ann Boroch "was actively campaigning for people to take control of their lives and reject Big Pharma's crippling products in favor of natural healing." *So, she was at odds with Big PhRMA. How much at odds?* At once Slater entered her mind's-eye.

At that point, Max's head was spinning. She still had no idea whether any of these contacts related to Jeff's murder, but she had to shake off her lingering discovery and trudge on. She called the next number with the area code for Jackson, Mississippi, to further confirm a theory that was fomenting.

"Hello." The receptionist at the helm this time was a male.

"Yes, I'm trying to get in touch with Dr. Russell Blaylock?"

"Excuse me; how did you get this number?"

"I'm calling regarding Senator Jeffrey Lance?"

"Hold on."

Max waited, even though she had no clue what to say should the doctor take the call.

"Dr. Blaylock asked that you leave your name and number. He'll return your call."

"Um, I'll call at another time. Thank you." Max hung up the phone at once. *At least he's not dead.* She soon realized how ridiculous her abrupt response was. Her phone number could easily be traced.

She looked up information on the doctor again and confirmed that he was a retired neurosurgeon who now devoted his full attention to promoting alternative treatments for neurological disorders. He claimed many disorders stemmed from the toxins in aspartame, MSG, and other food additives, along with pesticides. *So, essentially, he's an expert on nutrition and food toxins,* Max assessed. As she continued to read down the page, she picked up a reference to his newsletter titled *The Blaylock Wellness Report.* She clicked on the link.

The home page stated that Blaylock was a doctor "who is unafraid to challenge establishment thinking." But after Max scanned a few other sites, she discovered a remarkably different picture. "Very curious, the doctor is portrayed 'as a quack, a conspiracy theorist, and pseudoscience peddler.'" *Wonder how the FDA weighs in?* she thought, until she picked up on another countervailing opinion. *Hmm, this may be noteworthy. It seems Suzanne Somers is a great supporter of Blaylock.* Right away, Max googled Somers' book, *Knockout.* From the book's description, Somers detailed interviews she had conducted with a variety of doctors who cured cancer, without the use of drugs. One of those doctors was Blaylock. "This is a shocker!" she blurted out. "Dr. Stanislaw Burzysnki was another."

Max ran her finger along the phone list and immediately found the number with the 713 area code for Houston, Texas. She gave it an optimistic shot.

"The Burzysnki Clinic. May I help you?"

"I'd like to speak with Dr. Burzysnki?" Max wondered whether Jeff was visiting a clinic or a person. She held her breath.

"Dr. Stanislaw or Dr. Gregory?"

"Ah, Dr. Stanislaw."

"You must make an appointment?"

"I'm sorry, I'll have to call back at another time."

Max at once brought up the clinic's website and read from the screen. "They provide cutting-edge cancer treatments. What's this?" As she skimmed the article, she learned the doctor created something called antineoplastons, a reported cure for a form of brain cancer. She skipped to the next line and read the statement: "Quality control of the clinical trials in which the Burzynski Clinic participates is maintained by strict adherence to written study protocols that are FDA reviewed and Institutional Review Board (IRB) approved prior to patient enrollment." A few more paragraphs later she read: "Currently, new FDA-reviewed Phase II and III clinical trials utilizing Antineoplastons are undergoing Institutional Review Board (IRB) approval."

So, they seem to get along, she thought, until she dug even deeper and found out that since the early '90s the FDA had been pressuring the Texas Medical Board to revoke Burzynski's medical license. At the time, Big PhRMA had 25 gene-targeted cancer drugs on the market and the assumption was that Burzynski's cancer-curing breakthrough would funnel money out of the pockets of the pharmaceutical companies. Max stumbled on a quotation from the former FDA Bureau of Drugs Director, Dr. Richard Crout, that read: "I never have and never will approve a new drug to an individual, but only to a large pharmaceutical firm with unlimited finances."

Sounds as though the FDA has no intention of ever letting the clinical trials succeed. Her conclusions began to paint a dark web. Then Max's eye caught another passage from a *New York Times* review for the movie *Burzynski*. It read: "No one appears to contest the efficacy of his treatment. The problem, the film suggests, is a pharmaceutical industry with nothing to gain—and much to lose—from the introduction of a highly successful, nontoxic competitor to chemotherapy and radiation."

"So, Dr. Burzynski's plight continues. This is mind-blowing!" Max could not refrain from blurting out. "According to the FDA website, Burzynski Clinic had received a warning letter citing a list of infractions in December, 2013, after being inspected by the IRB." *It seems that there was additional correspondence in October, 2016, and May, 2017. Hmm, and the pot is still boiling.*

Max leaned back in her chair and let her mind churn as she reassessed the situation. *Jeff supposedly met with or spoke with four doctors, in four different cities across the US—all specializing in some form of alternative medicine. All on the FDA radar for one reason or another—and one committed suicide under suspicious circumstances.*

That revelation was devastating. But there was one more puzzling number on the phone listing—the one with an international country code that Max recognized. It was the code for Tokyo, Japan. *But why on his personal cell?* With a quick glance at her watch, she calculated it was eight-thirty in the morning in the Far East. "What the hell!" She dialed the number.

"Dr. Mizukami's office," answered the receptionist with the expected Asian accent.

"May I speak with the doctor?"

"I sorry, he travel out of country. You leave name, number; he return call."

"I'll call back. Thank you." Max still did not know what she was looking for precisely and, until she did, she would limit the number of returned calls. For the time being she would rely on her cyber partner. She googled "dr mizukami tokyo." On the screen, it displayed a link: https://www.beenefits.com/propolis-and-cancer.pdf, prefaced by "My experience for advanced cancer patients— *Beenefits.*"

"Man, oh, man!" She clicked on the link. "This is insane—Jeff was seeking a cure made from bee pollen—and then he's killed by a bee." She continued to skim the article in disbelief. Unfortunately, most of it made little sense.

In a rare moment, she resorted to shouting loudly. "Sam!"

Chapter 11

Beeeeszare

"What's going on?" Sam rushed into her office, astounded by her unusual method of communication.

"Two weeks ago, Jeff traveled to New Mexico to visit someone at an apiary. The day after he returned he contacted a doctor in Japan who was curing cancer with bee pollen using a plant I can barely pronounce—*Baccharis dracunculifolia*. Then, last week Jeff was killed with bee venom in a hotel in Brazil. Do you have any stinging conclusions?"

"Other than its *beeeeszare?*"

"Clever!—Wait just a minute."

Max hit a *speed dial* number on her phone. "Hey, Doc, do you still have the senator's body?"

"Yes, I was just about to ship it off to the mortuary."

"Did you find any growths or traces of a disease of any kind?"

"No, other than the erupted blood vessels. All organs were of normal weight with no signs of abnormality."

"I need a huge favor. I need you to check again."

"Max!"

"Doc, please."

"I'm not opening it up again. The best I can do is a full body scan to make sure I didn't miss anything. But as far as I'm concerned, it was an extremely healthy body before receiving a deadly injection."

Max cringed at the thought that Jeff was reduced to an *it, a body, a corpse, a thing.* She relied on what little religion she could conjure up, hoping his soul was in a better place. "Thanks, Doc! I owe you one."

"Back to you in an hour."

"What was that about?"

"Allison, Jeff's wife, suspected an affair. But maybe Jeff was suffering from a serious disease and was looking for a cure." *Not sure which is worse,* she thought.

"You think he was stung by the very thing that he believed was going to save him?"

"Let's wait until we hear from the coroner." Max checked her watch. "It will be another thirty minutes." She reluctantly switched to an even more unpleasant topic. "You know the funeral is tomorrow?"

"Are you going to be okay?" Sam assumed she would attend.

"I'll need to be strong for Allison, but I might need someone to prop me up. How do you feel about being my escort?" Max despised funerals. The vivid memory of her mother's funeral was still fresh in her mind, along with that horrible night a year later when her father was murdered. A night when she was swept into hiding by a stranger. Ironically, that stranger was seated in front of her today. Max understood that Sam was only protecting her, but it denied her the opportunity to lay her father to rest. She swore then that she would never attend another funeral.

"Max, nobody makes them tougher than you, but of course, I'll be there if that's what you want. Besides, I hear the senator served his country honorably, and for that I'd be delighted to pay tribute."

Her phone rang, breaking the solemn moment.

"It's the coroner. Give me a sec."

"Hey, Doc, what did you find out?"

"The scan showed nothing, Max. Just as I said; it was a healthy body before it received a deadly injection of venom beyond human capacity."

"There has to be something," she mumbled.

"What did you say?"

"Nothing, just talking to myself. Have you notified the Capitol Police?"

"No, that was next on my list."

"Do you think you can hold off until after the funeral tomorrow? It's at nine in the morning."

"Max, you know I can't send the corpse to the mortuary,

knowing the cause of death is murder without reporting it."

"I need to be the one to tell his wife. Allison doesn't need the chief throwing questions at her right now. Just give us a day."

"Don't ask me again. I can't do this one for you. You better call her now."

The line went dead.

"Shit!"

"No go?" From her sourpuss expression, it was obvious to Sam that she didn't get her way.

"It's not over yet. Hold on." Max hit another *speed dial* button.

"Hey, Ray."

"What do you want, Max?" The Capitol Police chief knew the familiar tone on the other end of the line. It always came with a bespoke catch.

"The coroner is about to call you to tell you that Senator Jeffrey Lance's death was not caused by a heart attack, but was murder. I want you to hold the information until after the funeral tomorrow."

"I don't even want to know how you get your information. But what's your interest in this case—assuming there is a case?"

"Jeff was a close friend. I want to be the one to tell his wife, who is my dearest friend. But not until after the funeral."

"And that's it?" the chief asked, overcome with that unsettled feeling he gets when Max is involved.

"That's it—promise!"

"Let Mrs. Lance know I'll be paying her a visit tomorrow afternoon around three."

"Thanks, Chief. You're the best."

Ray heard the click. He knew she was lying through her pearly whites. He also knew she would most likely come up with something he could use to his advantage. *In the information-trading game, favors came with a price.* He beamed at the thought.

Max sat back with a self-assured expression, although she expected the chief would hound her later for information. But she got what she wanted for the moment.

"Your tenacity knows no bounds." Sam shook his head.

Max grinned, accepting what she deemed a compliment. Then she shut down her computer, feigned a yawn, and announced, "It's late, and I'm officially calling it a night. By the way, my flight to New Mexico leaves on Saturday morning."

"You're really following up on the apiary caper? As your newly beloved partner, I can go check it out for you."

"Thanks, but this will be easy-peasy. I just want to find out why they closed the business in Clovis. I'll be back in the office on Monday."

"Max knows best." Sam smiled and then in a more solemn tone, asked, "What time did you say the funeral begins?"

"Nine."

"I'll make the coffee."

"Strong, please. And thanks for being here."

"Hey, kid, I think this is the beginning of a beautiful friendship."

"Play it again, Sam." Max gave a relaxed chuckle and then said, "C'mon, let's get you settled in."

Chapter 12

The Funeral Procession

The somber funeral matched the gray December sky looming over the Arlington National Cemetery. The full military gun salute only added to the solemnity in the air that reverberated throughout the Capitol city. It was a great tribute to Senator Jeffrey Lance with President Post in attendance, along with many members of Congress. While delivering the eulogy, the president lauded the senator's bravery as a military hero and recipient of two Bronze Stars received during his tours in Afghanistan and Iraq. He praised the senator for continuing his fight for the betterment of the American people in the U.S. Congress. In his closing statement, President Post said, Senator Lance's death "was a true heartbreak for our nation."

It was impressive to see members from both sides of the aisle paying tribute, although Max thought it was sad that it took a tragedy to bring them together. She also suspected they would be out for each other's jugular by sundown. *How unfortunate for the American people*, she thought. Then another jugular came to mind, noting Noble's absence. Sam stood by her side as promised, but it did not stop that tiny bubble of anger from erupting inside. She knew at some point she would have to let the anger go—for now she refocused on Allison. All her angst was minor compared to what her dearest friend was enduring.

The newly minted widow stared straight ahead as two soldiers folded America's precious symbol that moments earlier draped the coffin. Then with trembling hands, Allison received the flag and clutched it against her chest. As the coffin slowly descended into the dark earth, she wept uncontrollably.

Max felt helpless. She reached over and placed her hand on her friend's shoulder, but the gesture seemed inadequate and hollow.

Sam noticed. "Are you okay?" he whispered.

Max nodded and inhaled, trying to fight back her own tears. The funeral was over, but the military protocol reintroduced bitter memories of her father's life and his honor that had been robbed. She could hear Daniel and her father argue vividly in the recesses of her mind. The sounds of gunshots still rang in her ears. She shivered.

Sam felt the tremor as his arm pressed against hers. He reached over to hold her hand.

Stanton, standing near the president, noticed as well. He ached to be the one to console her, but knew it was too soon after Noble's tragic death. Her nerves were still raw; he would give her the time she needed to heal. *But who's that guy with her?* he wondered.

Fortunately, the site of the president being escorted by hordes of agents, signaled others in attendance that the service had officially ended.

"I'm going with Allison in the limo. I'll meet you at their home."
Max was visibly ready to leave.

"You okay?"

"I'm fine. Stop asking."

"Then I'll see you shortly." Sam headed for the Uber, parked
and waiting.

Allison remained trance-like still clasping the flag.

"Sweetie, we have to go now," Max urged.

There was no response. She remained frozen in her seat. But
with help from her children, they finally managed to escort Allison
back to the limo. Silence prevailed during the twenty-minute drive
from the cemetery to the senator's family home, located only a few
blocks from Max's Victorian, near Lincoln Park.

As anticipated, the Lances' home was filled with family, close friends,
and colleagues. They were marking time by helping themselves to
the catered affair of breakfast foods. Fortunately, during the quiet
ride home, Allison pulled herself together enough to mingle with
the crowd as they each paid their respects for a second time. The
children wasted no time to gather plates of food and retire to their
rooms. Computer games gave them the needed distraction from the
day's events. But within the hour, Allison became noticeably tired.

Max put off the inevitable, but now she had to inform Allison
that the police chief would arrive in a few hours to bombard her
with the usual banal questions. As she laid out her game plan, she
spotted Sam in the corner chomping on a bagel.

He spotted her heading his way.

"Do you mind working the room? Encourage everyone to leave."

Sam checked his watch; it was approaching noon. "I'll take care of them—good luck with Allison."

"Thanks! I'll meet you back at the office."

Chapter 13

A Rude Awakening

The house was quiet, and Max and Allison were finally alone. Now she had to face her dear friend and relay the tragic news. Death was difficult enough to grasp; murder was beyond the pale. Max had a little time to spare and chose to take it slow.

"My dear, how are you holding up?" Max asked.

"Horribly. You want some wine?"

"Why not?! It's five o'clock somewhere. I'll go pour us a glass; you go relax."

Max was delighted to oblige. She needed a glass herself. While she walked into the kitchen, Allison walked over and sat down on the sofa. Minutes later, they were sharing fond memories and toasting Jeff.

"I know this is a horrible time, but we need to talk," Max insisted.

"What's so important that it can't wait? I'd really like to sit here and just sip on my wine."

Max hated to ignore her plea, but she had no choice. But first, there was something else she needed to know. Ignoring her original purpose for the moment, she asked, "Was Jeff ill?"

Allison recoiled. "Why would you ask that?"

Max picked up on her reaction and decided to use a careful, measured tone. "For the past several months, Jeff either spoke with or met with a series of doctors practicing alternative medicine. These appointments appeared not to be part of his official duties, but of a personal nature," she explained, sharing what she had uncovered thus far.

Allison shook her head, still trying to grasp all that had happened. "I guess it doesn't matter anymore."

"What doesn't matter?"

"A year and a half ago, Jeff was diagnosed with pancreatic cancer..."

"Why didn't you tell me?" Max could not refrain from interrupting and started to sound more as a friend and less of a detective.

"It was Jeff's wishes. It happened during the previous campaign, and he assumed it would hurt his chances for reelection."

"The last time I saw him he was in great shape. It was obvious he had lost a little weight, but I thought it was intentional. His spirits were certainly high."

"That's what's so amazing! One year later, he was deemed cancer-free. Max, he was in perfect health. And after everything our family endured—he ends up dying of a fucking heart attack. I don't buy it!" Allison's grief instantly changed to understandable anger.

"Pancreatic cancer is a death sentence," Max said, harboring doubts, recalling stats she had run across in the past. "Isn't the survival rate around twenty percent?"

"That was my understanding when the doctor broke the news. Then we came to learn it was frighteningly lower if not caught early." Allison hesitated. "The idea of losing someone I loved so dearly became unimaginable."

Unfortunately, Max could empathize, although she still did not understand how he survived. "But…"

Allison cut her short and continued, "We researched endlessly for a cure. We ended up meeting with thirteen oncologists and six doctors who practice alternative medicine. Each oncologist offered similar procedures of chemotherapy, surgery, and then radiation in varying degrees, but in the end, everyone agreed that surgery was a necessary first step."

"So, Jeff agreed to have the surgery?"

"Yes, he assumed that if there was something in his body that didn't belong there, it should be taken out. It was a fairly easy decision to have the cancer cells, which had metastasized, removed. Naturally, we understood the inherent dangers of surgery, but we felt it was worth the risk. However, Jeff was vehemently opposed when it came to any chemo or radiation therapy."

Max marveled at how Allison had morphed from a grieving widow to an articulate educator, well versed on the subject matter. And while she listened intently, she glanced periodically across the room, noting the hands on the Grandfather clock. Soon, Max would have to prepare Allison, bringing her back to the realism of the day. But with a bit more time to spare before the chief arrived, she was curious to know how Jeff beat the odds.

"Isn't it assumed that Jeff reduced his likelihood of survival without some form of chemo or radiation?"

"In these matters, Jeff always considered himself the client and that the doctors were there to serve him. When we met with the various health practitioners, he grilled them with questions. Ultimately, to his credit, he decided to take a mixed approach. Jeff had the surgery to remove the tumor, along with seventeen lymph nodes for added insurance. But as I said, he refused the radiation and chemotherapy protocol. We came to understand that it not only kills the cancer cells, but it kills the healthy stem cells, decreasing the number of white blood cells that compromise the immune system. That's why the cancer returns and often spreads to other organs. In fact, one in three cancer survivors will get a second cancer. In many cases, the reoccurrence is linked to certain chemotherapies and high doses of radiation. Max, all of us have cancer cells in our body. After years of bathing them in toxic chemicals found in our food and personal care products—they're lying in wait to metastasize. But Jeff learned of a way to stop it in its tracks."

"In what way?" Max ignored the time, suddenly fascinated by Allison's knowledge.

"He followed a more holistic approach using nature's products instead of toxic cancer drugs. He started by juicing with organic vegetables that contain no preservatives. It was essential to detoxing his body before surgery. He also took several supplements to boost his immune system, as prescribed by what he liked to call his voodoo doctor. Then, he simply changed his diet going forward. He avoided white flour and sugar and removed other synthetic and refined foods from his regimen. You'd be amazed at the number of products as commonplace as olive oil, garlic and green tea that are anticancer products. Science shows that with a healthy routine, you can literally, stop the cancer stem cells from absorbing the exact elements that caused them to grow into killer cells."

"This is so incredible." Max was astounded.

"No, it's by the grace of God—it truly was a miracle. But Jeff's message should be loud and clear. We shouldn't wait until we get cancer to figure out which route to go. Have you ever heard the name David Servan-Schrieber?"

Max shook her head, encouraging Allison to continue.

"He was a French psychiatrist, who at the age of thirty-one, was diagnosed with brain cancer. He had the tumor removed, but it returned. Having already gone through radiation and chemotherapy, he opted for a natural, holistic treatment only as a supplement. Jeff was drawn to the benefits of a diet and nutrition that Servan-Schrieber championed. Sadly, he died last July at the age of fifty, after surviving almost twenty years. But he had written several books, one titled *Anticancer: A New Way of Life*, and it opened our eyes. It's a fascinating read; it might even get you to adopt a healthier lifestyle."

"No thanks, and as engrossing as this information is, there's one thing I still don't understand. Why would Jeff still be meeting with doctors practicing alternative medicine if he were completely cancer-free?"

"Trust me. I sat in on all of his appointments and I can testify the cancer was gone. It had been completely eradicated. But what happened to Jeff had a profound effect on him, even though he didn't talk about it a lot. Except one time he mentioned a Dr. Bradstreet and said he was working on something. Then, Jeff mentioned his name again. It was right before he left on his last trip. He said he needed to make sure it would never happen again. Something about stopping the insanity and getting Congress to recognize alternative medicine."

"I still don't understand."

"I didn't either. After his near-death experience I expected he'd spend more time at home with me and the kids, but his travels accelerated. I asked him why, but he blew it off as being work-related. I got the sense that he thought he had already said too much, so I didn't press further. I don't know what was going on with him."

I'd say he was on a personal quest. But what was it? What got him killed? Answers to those questions will have to wait. "Allison, I'm amazed by everything you've told me." Max contemplated for a second and then asked, "Would you text me a list of the alternative doctors that you and Jeff met with?"

"Why?"

"I'm just following up on a hunch. Right now, there's something else we need to discuss."

"Max, not now. I'm exhausted and I'm going to go lie down."

There's only one way to say it. "There's proof that Jeff was murdered."

Allison was stunned into silence.

Max was not sure if she was dumbfounded or in shock. "Did you hear me?"

Allison ignored her question, got up and walked into the bedroom. Max still needed to tell her that the police chief would arrive within the hour to speak with her. But within moments, Allison returned with an odd expression. She was carrying one of Jeff's shirts.

"Here! Explain this. It was in Jeff's belongings that were sent back from Brazil."

Max looked at the lipstick-smudged shirt that still reeked of cheap perfume. She recalled Sam's description of the murder scene in the hotel room and then thought how stupid the local authorities were to mail the shirt back to his widow.

"Allison, I assure you Jeff was not having an affair. He was working on something—exactly what I'm not sure, but I will find out. What I can tell you is that Sam spoke with the desk clerk at the hotel and he said that Jeff received no visitors. Most likely, whoever murdered him was already waiting in his room and made it look like something it was not. Was Jeff's phone among his belongings?" Max was hoping for possibly text messages that would have not shown up in the cell phone records.

"No. Other than his clothing. Oh, his briefcase and wallet were empty, and his passport was missing."

"The State Department probably has the passport."

"This is too much to bear right now. Max, I really want to be alone."

"I'm sorry dear, but in about thirty minutes, Chief Ray Tomson of the Capitol Police will be showing up to speak with you."

"What does he want from me?" she cried.

"It's just routine."

"Max, you handle it!"

"Trust me; I'm the last person the chief will let hang around while he speaks with you. Just answer his questions. But Allison—there's no need to mention Jeff's bout with cancer—or the shirt. In fact, why don't you let me take it."

Allison returned to her zombie state and handed Max the shirt. "I'm going to lie down." She reached over, hugged Max and then turned and walked back toward her bedroom.

"I promise you, I will find out what happened. Just call me if you need anything." Max's overture fell on deaf ears.

After Allison's retreat, Max left with what might be evidence, although she suspected the real evidence had been stolen to make it appear to be a robbery.

Chapter 14

The Common Denominator

Max strode into Sam's office. It was obvious she was on edge as she leaned against the door frame. "Hey."

"Hey, yourself. How did it go with Allison?"

"As you might expect. The chief will be showing up at her home anytime now." Max's oral response did not align with her facial expression.

Sam noticed Max's mien. It usually indicated she was about to wade deeper into the weeds. "What is it?" he asked, in an apprehensive tone.

She pulled up a chair and sat down. "Jeff had pancreatic cancer."

"Seriously?"

"Wait—there's more. Over six months ago, he was given a clean bill of health. Cancer gone."

Sam remained quiet as he contemplated the odds of survival and then asked the gnawing question. "Why did he reach out to alternative medicine practitioners in the last six months—after he was cured?"

"That's the question before the house. I asked Allison. She said something having to do with a Dr. Bradstreet and him never wanting it to happen again."

"Jeffrey Bradstreet?"

"I don't know—why?"

"If he's the same guy, he was infamous for railing against vaccines. Watch these magic fingers." Sam winked as he tapped away at the keyboard.

Max waited patiently for his brilliant discovery.

"Abracadabra! Bradstreet discovered a natural occurring protein that not only cured neurological impairment, but also cancer. The protein is called GcMAF. It stands for Globulin component Macrophage Activating Factor. Don't ask me what that means. Oh, wait a minute. This says it's an essential human protein our bodies make naturally and aids in removing several diseases, including cancer. Evidently, the problem is that an enzyme called nagalase is introduced into the body through vaccinations, according to Bradstreet, and is secreted by cancer cells that block the activating factor in the Globulin component Macrophage, thus resulting in seriously compromising the immune system!"

"So, GcMAF is a replacement therapy for the body when it stops producing the cancer-killing protein on its own?" Max asked.

"That's my take."

"Hey, I remember now, Bradstreet used GcMAF to treat cases of autism. That would explain why he was so anti-vaccine."

"Yeah, but the problem is—GcMAF is banned in the US."

"Why is it banned?"

"It was being manufactured from human blood and dispensed online by a UK company called Immuno Biotech headquartered in the Channel Islands; the brand name is called First Immune. They claim the UK's version of the FDA, the Medicines and Healthcare Products Regulatory Agency, or MHRA, was trying to put them out of business. So much so, they've had Immuno Biotech's scientist and doctors fired and their CEO, David Noakes, arrested."

"I still don't understand. Why is it banned?"

"All I know is what it says here; it's highly illegal. The FDA issued a statement to the *Washington Post* saying that 'GcMAF treatments are considered investigational, and none are approved or licensed for use by the FDA in the U.S.' They discredit Bradstreet's research, but apparently his supporters, on both sides of the pond, point to the huge pharmaceutical corporations and their bottom lines."

"Maybe that's why Jeff was meeting with Slater so much. Perhaps, negotiating a deal."

Sam's expression conveyed one of doubt. But he continued to search for information and left Max to contemplate.

"Wait—here's more!" Sam exclaimed. "Four months after they finally shut down Immuno Biotech, Bradstreet's clinic in Buford, Georgia was raided by federal agents looking specifically for GcMAF. In the same *Washington Post* article, it states that if Bradstreet had been indicted, he would have faced up to twenty years in prison. Days later he was found dead in the Rocky Broad River in North Carolina. Reports say it was a self-inflicted gunshot wound to the chest. But not everyone buys it, including David

Noakes, who continues to be embroiled in legal troubles. However, he continues to stand by Bradstreet's patient successes, and contends that he was murdered. Here's a reference to a woman by the name of Erin Elizabeth, who also dismisses the cause of death as suicide. Evidently, she has a website called 'Health Nut News.'"

"I think I ran across that name before." Max used her phone to check it out. Within a matter of seconds, she located the site and flipped down the home page. "Wow, Erin's really into this stuff; health, fitness, beauty, environment."

"Admired by a woman who eats greasy croissants," Sam snickered.

"I have a great metabolism," she rebuffed.

"If you continue to dump all that fat and sugar into your body, your metabolism will be the least of your problems. Remind me to buy you a copy of Michael Moss's book, *Salt Sugar Fat.*"

"Enlighten me."

"He's a Pulitzer Prize-winning investigative reporter for the *New York Times*. That's only one of his books, but it discusses how the food industry giants blatantly ignored the growing obesity epidemic. Instead, they concentrate on making unhealthy food taste good, so 'you can't eat just one.' Seemed like an innocent jingle at the time when Lay's Potato Chips first came out with it; not so much these days."

"Are we now indicting the *Food Giants*?"

"Remember what the 'F' in FDA stands for?"

"And when did you become such a *health nut* anyway?—if I may use the term."

Sam shrugged his shoulders. He knew he was getting off point, but it was hard to ignore, including the manipulation for profit that hovered over ordinary lives. "Health nut? Since you've had me studying up on these doctors, it does cause one to reflect on lifestyle decisions through a different prism. It's compelling stuff; you have to admit."

"Listen; now back to Erin Elizabeth. It appears she has become an activist in reporting on a series of deaths of doctors that had connections to alternative health medicine. Hmm, this is attention-grabbing. She's also producing a movie called *The Power to Cure,* depicting what happened to none other than Bradstreet. She states that investigators have concluded without a doubt that he was murdered."

"Hmm, is right." Sam agreed, but he could tell something else was on her mind. "What's going through that gorgeous head of yours?"

Max had already scrolled down the home page and spotted the report of one of the deceased doctors. "Remember Ann Boroch, the naturopathic doctor from L.A.—the one who supposedly hanged herself in her garage in August?"

"Yeah. Didn't she have a reputation for operating—shall we say—outside the confines of Big PhRMA?"

"Sam, Jeff visited her three days before she took her life. Now, we have to wonder what the other doctors were up to."

"Easy, Max; I see a conspiracy developing."

"Hey, while I'm gone, will you check to see if there are any links between Bradstreet and the other doctors Jeff contacted?

Something smells, and the stench is wafting between Big PhRMA and the FDA. Then of course, there's Clovis Hill."

"You mean the apiary?"

"Yeah, I'm more than curious to find out why it was closed shortly after Jeff's visit. Conspiracy?—I honestly don't know."

"Maybe that's the common denominator."

"What?—bee venom." She smirked and then realized Sam may have hit on something.

"Hey, it's a possible connection."

"There's got to be something else. What was Jeff talking about? Not wanting what to happen again? Could it be harassment by the FDA—or worse?" Max was finding her own words a bit frightening.

"We'll get the answers, princess. I'll find out what I can. It might be worthwhile to contact Erin Elizabeth directly to see what she has to say. You never know. By the way, what time is your flight tomorrow morning?"

"It's at eight-thirty. I booked a car with Carmel."

"Not an Uber fan?"

"No! I'll be back on Monday. Just find any links you can."

"Don't worry, I'll keep plenty *beezy.*"

"Cut with the *apilinguistics.*"

Chapter 15

Max Goes To Clovis

The plane arrived on schedule at the Clovis Municipal Airport in Texico, New Mexico. It was three o'clock in the afternoon, with three hours of daylight left to spare. Max hurried off to pick up the rental car and exited the airport onto NM-525 W and headed to Curry Road. From the air, Clovis looked like a patchwork quilt, but at eye level the land was flat and barren as far as the eye could see. Only a few homes dotted the landscape. Seventeen minutes down a straight highway, she spotted a sign marked "Clovis Hill Apiary." She turned on to a dirt road and drove a half mile up a belly-bump of a hill until she arrived at a government-issued, chain-link fence. The only entryway was locked by an even heavier chain and padlock. Everything seemed out of place as did the large ominous sign plastered on the gate: **WARNING Restricted Area. It is unlawful to enter this property without permission.** Most troubling were the words: **Use of deadly force authorized.**

The yellow tape added concern, but Max was undeterred. She had not come all that way to turn around and go home none the wiser. "I doubt I'll be shot for standing outside," she concluded. And knowing her Sig Sauer was tucked inside her handbag gave her reassurance. But still she used caution when stepping outside the car and walking toward the gate. Roughly fifty feet away, she spotted an old white stone building with a slanting gray roof. The attached garage had two large steel doors. There was no evidence of wooden hives lying around, but she assumed they were stacked behind the building structure.

"Hey, lady, no trespassin'!"

The crotchety voice startled Max until she saw the squat figure bounding toward her. *This guy has all the classic traits of a rent-a-cop,* she thought. Sizing him up as less than a threat, she asked, "Excuse me, I was just curious as to why the apiary was closed."

"You take that up with the Curry County Sheriff. Now git."

"Just one more question—is this a crime scene?" Max pointed to the yellow tape.

"Y'all city folk always pokin' your nose in where it dudden belong. Now, I sed git!" The disturbing creature shooed her away with the motion of his hand, then turned and lumbered back toward the building.

"Charming. Looks like it's time for plan 'B.'" Back inside the car, Max typed 'curry county sheriff' into the GPS. "Perfect, only eighteen minutes away." Her foot hit the gas pedal.

The Curry County Courthouse on Main Street took little effort to find, including the nearest parking space in front of the main entrance. Upon entering the red brick building, Max easily located suite number four with the words "Sheriff's Office" stenciled on the glass door. When she entered, she saw three of the towns finest seated before her, all gawking at the newcomer in town.

"Ma'am, can I help you?" asked the deputy seated at the nearest desk.

It was obvious the other ears in the room were piqued.

"May I speak with the sheriff?"

"Ma'am, what brung you to our lovely town?"

"The sheriff, please."

"Of course, but I'll need to tell him who—and why—you wanna' speak with him," he said in a long irritating drawl.

Max, frustrated at his attempt to string her along, decided to pull out all verbal guns and throw around enough clout to settle him down. "My name is not Ma'am, it's Max Ford. I'm a private investigator from Washington, DC, and I'd like to speak with the sheriff about the Clovis Hill Apiary."

"Not sure he can help you much. The Feds took that over when they swooped in and locked it up."

"The sheriff, please." Max stood her ground. She recognized her attire made her stand out from the local crowd. There was no time to go to the hotel to change. Time was of the essence. And little did she realize, the sheriff had listened to the entire inquisition from inside his office, but chose to let his deputies have their fun.

After several chuckles, he finally poked his head out and asked, "May, I help you? I'm Sheriff Wesley Waller."

Max was thrown for a loop. The sheriff was surprisingly attractive. His six-foot slim frame, with gray hair topping a youngish face, was nothing like the yahoos she had seen in town since her arrival.

The deputy caught the look on her face and interjected. "This little lady's a PI *all-the-way* from our nation's capital. She'd be wantin' to talk with you bout Clovis Hill." That time his southern drawl was laced with curiosity.

"Thank you, Mike. But I bet she could have said that all by herself." The sheriff waved Max into his office as the others in the room razzed the bemused deputy.

"Please excuse 'em," he apologized. Then, brandishing a charming smile, he pulled up a chair next to his desk and offered her a seat. "Now, what can I do for you?"

"I'm working on a case that led me to the Clovis Hill Apiary. Can you please tell me why it was closed?"

"Nope, not a clue." He shook his head in honest dismay. "It was the strangest thing. In less than twenty-four hours of Miss Ellie findin' poor Ollie dead, the Feds circled in and shut down the whole place."

"I'm sorry, but who are these people?"

"The Princes. Oliver Prince was the owner of the apiary. His poor wife was the one who found 'im dead in a swarm of bees."

"The beekeeper died from bee stings?" Max could hardly believe her ears.

"Some coincidence, ain't it."

"What actually happened?"

"Accordin' to Miss Ellie, she was waitin' for old Ollie to arrive for supper. You see she runs the office from their home at the apiary. The converted garage was the warehouse and laboratory. Out back was the bee hives. I reckon they had over fifty hives. That's a million bees, give or take a few buzzers. And their honey was as pure and sweet as y'all ever find in these parts..."

"Please, Sheriff, what happened?" Max's impatience became obvious.

"Oh, sorry, I do get carried away. Anyway, Ollie was endin' a tour he was givin' to a group of students. Miss Ellie saw the students leavin', so she expected him to arrive at the table on time. She waited on him bout another fifteen minutes, then she went to fetch him. Right inside the door to the lab, lay poor Ollie covered with bees. Miss Ellie called for an ambulance, but it was too late."

"Did you speak with the..."

"Yeees, we spoke with the students, confirmin' Ollie was alive and well when they left."

"Reading my mind?"

"In our business it helps."

"You wouldn't possibly have the coroner's report?"

"Sure thing." The sheriff looked toward the door and called out the order. "Hey, Mike, go fetch me the Prince file." Then he returned his attention to Max, trying to size her up, wondering what she was really looking for.

Max sensed she was being examined under a microscope. *Thank heavens*, she thought when the deputy burst into the office.

"Here you go, Sheriff," he said, and then managed a wink in Max's direction before he departed.

What's with that guy?

"Here it is. Ollie was stung forty times. The tox report show two-hundred milligrams of apitoxin in his bloodstream, I guess that means bee venom."

"It does, and it's enough to cause anaphylactic shock. He most likely suffocated." Max's mental calculator moved into gear. *Forty stings would only inject a total of four milligrams. Both Jeff and Ollie died from the same exact dose.* "It doesn't add up. He would have had to

die literally of a thousand stings—more or less, given his weight."
Oh, my God, Sam was right.

"Forty opposite a thousand is a whole lot different. Are you suggestin'..."

Max cut him off that time. "Yes!"

"What's your interest in this case, anyhow?

"A friend died in Brazil from an injection of two-hundred milligrams of apitoxin."

"The same amount as old Ollie?" the sheriff asked in disbelief.

"That friend also visited the apiary a few weeks before his death. I don't believe it's a coincidence."

"So, what's those Feds got to do with this?"

"That's what I'd like to know."

"Dang, we got ourselves a gen-u-ine murder mystery goin' on here."

"I'd like to speak with Mrs. Prince. Do you know how I can contact her?"

"Sure, Miss Ellie's stayin' with her sister just down the road a piece. I mentioned the apiary was their home, but once those Feds showed up they kicked her out, only allowin' her to collect a few of her things. Heartless, I say." The sheriff reached for a piece of paper and jotted down the address for Ellie Prince. "Here you go. And you find out anything, I'd appreciate it if you'd pass it along."

"I will, Sheriff. You've been most helpful." Max stood up to leave.

"Ma'am, please let me escort you pass all those sniffin' hounds." The charming smile returned.

"Thank you." Max appreciated his southern hospitality, despite the protracted means it took to get to the next piece of the puzzle.

Chapter 16

Good On 'Em

The GPS squawked a series of straightforward directions in a town that seemed laid out in a straightforward grid. It only took twenty minutes, heading away from Clovis back to Texico, before Max spotted a meager pueblo-style home off the main highway. She turned left onto the dirt road and drove slowly toward the house. All seemed quiet. She rapped on the door a few times and prayed Mrs. Prince would be home. While she stood waiting, she took the opportunity to surveil the rundown property.

In Max's usual curious style, she had read up on this quaint town on her flight over. Everything looked as expected: flat and desolate. With a population of a tad over eleven hundred, Texico lay on New Mexico's border, sharing its boundary with Farwell, Texas. The entire town was only point-eight square miles, resting on the high plains.

"May I help you?" asked the elderly woman.

"Mrs. Prince?"

"Oh no, you be wantin' Miss Ellie. Can I tell her who come to call?"

"My name is Max Ford, and I'm working on a case that may be connected to Mr. Prince's death. The Sheriff gave me this address."

"Sheriff Wesley! Why didn't you say that in the first place? C'mon in, I'll git Miss Ellie."

Max remained standing in the living room overrun with Native furnishings, until a slightly younger woman, bearing family traits, entered the room.

"You wanna talk about Ollie?" asked Miss Ellie in a soft, gentle manner.

"Mrs. Prince, my condolences for the loss of your husband."

"Thank you, my dear. And call me Miss Ellie, everyone else in these here parts do. Now, please join me and tell me what you know about Ollie's passin'." Miss Ellie sat down, and Max joined her on the sofa.

"Only what the sheriff told me, but it may somehow be related to the death of a dear friend."

"Oh, my." Miss Ellie seemed confused.

"This must be extremely painful, but would you mind telling me exactly what happened that evening?"

"Well, dear, I wuz waitin' for Ollie to wrap up his work and come to supper. That wuz the day he gave a tour to a group of young'uns wantin' to be apiarists. You know dear, those wantin' to breed bees. If I do recall, it wuz about five-thirty when I saw the students leavin'. Oh, my, there wuz that man..."

"A man?"

"Yes, he arrived right before the young'uns left. He dudden have an appointment, but he wuz wantin' to speak with Ollie. He said it won't take but just a minute. I called Ollie and told him, but he sed the man should wait in our little reception room until he finished the tour."

Max noticed an odd look wash over Miss Ellie's face.

"Strangest thing. When those young'uns were leavin', I went to tell the man, but he'd already left."

"Left to go where."

"Well, I reckoned to go see Ollie. So, I wuz just waitin' on him for supper. I feel so foolish now. I shudda gone out there mah self."

"Can you describe the man?" Max thought it best to get all she could before asking the last highly-intrusive question.

"I think he wuz a little taller than you. His hair wuz darker too, more sandy-brown. Caint remember the color of his eyes. Maybe cause I caint take my eyes off that nasty scar on his left cheek."

"A scar. Was it jagged? Was it straight?"

"Oh, it wuz straight, just like this." She used her index finger to draw an imaginary line straight from the edge of her outer eye to the edge of her lip. "Nasty thing."

"Miss Ellie, I'm sorry to ask you this, but could you please tell me what happened when you found your husband?" Max could see tears welling up in her eyes, but the answer could be of vital importance.

"It wuz a God-awful sight. Those bees swarmin' all over him. I went to fetch the smoker as fast I could to calm 'em down. But it wuz too late, they already stung poor Ollie to death."

"How could that have happened? Mr. Prince must have known how to handle the bees."

"Ollie's not the careless sort. But it looked like he had been workin' in the lab with one of those frames from the hives. I have no idea why he whudda or what he'd been doin' with it, but all it takes is for one sting to release them pheromones. Any bees buzzin' around go on the attack. You know, it's their natural instinct to want to protect the hive, even though it's rare for a honey bee to sting you. But that must've been what happen'd." She sniffled and then asked in a weakened tone, "Is that what happen'd to your friend?"

"Something like that. I'm surprised the sheriff never mentioned the man that came to see Ollie."

"Oh my, perhaps I plumb forgot. That wuz a horrible time and I wuz frettin' for help."

Max noticed a sheepish expression on Miss Ellie's cherubic face. "Is there something else you forgot to mention to the sheriff?"

"Well, I dudden know what Ollie wuz messin' with, but he told me that if anythin' happen'd to him that I shud wash his drive. And I ought not to tell no one."

"You mean scrub the hard drive on his computer?"

"Yes, ma'am, that's it. I don't know much bout that stuff, but he show'd me how to do it."

"So, all the documents, data, his appointment schedules—everything he was working on—has been erased?"

"Everythin' but his appointment schedule; I got that right here. I told you I don't know much bout that computer stuff, so I write everything down. You think I done right? Because those mean ol' government men kicked me outta my own home. That just ain't fittin'. Good on 'em, I say."

"How did the Feds become aware that your husband had died?"

"No idea. A few hours later, when I returned from the morgue, they were there and had everythin' locked up. I had to plead with them to let me fetch a few of mah personal things. Imagine that—I had to plead."

Max did not push; it was another dot with nothing to connect to for the moment. "Would it be possible for me to borrow the appointment calendar? I promise to return it to you."

"Well, it don't do me no good now. If it'll help you find out what happen'd to your friend, I suppose so. You wait right here now."

While Max waited, she remembered something else. *It might be a long shot,* she thought, *but what the hell?*

"Here you go, dear."

"Miss Ellie, do you ever recall a man, around six feet, two inches tall with blond hair and blue eyes? He might even be Scandinavian."

Clearly, the wheels were turning. "That sounds like that Sorenson fella. He wuz from the Food and Drug Administration. At first, I thought he wuz nosin' around checkin' on the quality of our honey. But he been showin' up quite a bit here. I think Ollie took a shine to him."

With Max's antennae fully extended, she described Jeff. Miss Ellie also confirmed what she suspected. Jeff had met with the beekeeper.

"Is there anyone else that stands out. Someone who visited frequently?"

"Well, it's usually rather quiet around here. But this last year, there's been a lot people poppin' in. Not locals, they're more refined folk like yourself."

"Miss Ellie, I don't want to take any more of your time. And once again, my condolences."

"My pleasure, dear. I hope I've been helpful."

Max assured the lovely lady that she had been more than cooperative, even though Max didn't exactly understand how it all added up, except for one conclusion—Jeff and the beekeeper were killed by the same person.

Chapter 17

Sam Comes to Clovis

Max was dog-tired. But armed with encouraging evidence and no time to spare, she punched in the directions on the GPS and headed to her hotel. Once back on the familiar streets of Clovis, she spotted the neon sign up ahead for the Super 8 Motel. Just past that were the golden arches. Exhaustion, mixed with starvation, steered the car first to the drive-in window to retrieve a southwestern grilled chicken salad and a large coffee—an appeasement for all the previous Big Macs. Once checked into the motel, she had one more thing to do before settling in for the night—place a call.

"Hey, Max. What's happening?" Sam's voice betrayed his attempt to hide his eagerness.

"I'll fill you in when you get here."

"Get where?" He asked, even though his instincts told him he was not going to like the answer.

"Clovis—and you will never believe this; the owner of the apiary was killed by a swarm of bee stings."

"What?!"

"Listen to this. The tox report showed the identical level of apitoxin found in Jeff's bloodstream—and once they discovered the beekeeper's body—they shut down the whole place—lock, stock, and beehive."

"Why would the local authorities close the apiary?"

"Guess again?"

"The ever-loving Feds?!"

"You got it! That's why I need you to burrow your way in and find out why. Bring a fake ID and a large briefcase. You can never tell what you'll uncover."

"Whoa, hold your horses! What have you gotten yourself into this time? And excuse me; you're just as capable of breaking in as I am. What's the old adage? 'If you don't use your spy skills, you'll lose your spy skills.'"

"Ha-ha, but I can't. They've got this old, crotchety rent-a-cop who won't budge. C'mon, Sam, I need you on this one."

Sam was spinning alternatives in his head, but none morphed into likely possibilities.

"Sam! This is what you signed up for partner."

After a slight hesitation he caved. "Okay, princess, you win. I'll see you tomorrow. Where're you staying?"

"The Super 8."

"Wonderful," he moaned. "Get me a room."

"Ah Sam, when the lights are out, they all look the same."

"I'll grab the same flight you took. Pick me up?"

"Sure, I'll see you at three. And thanks, you're a life saver."

"I hope it doesn't come to that! Gotta go. Arrangements to make."

Now with that settled, Max took a serious stab at both her McDonald's salad and the beekeeper's appointment calendar.

Chapter 18

The Apiary Caper

The scheduled flight arrived on time, so Max waited at the curb. When she saw Sam exit the modest building that sufficed as a terminal, she flashed her headlights to gain his attention. Catching the glimmer, he headed toward the car, carrying an oversized briefcase. Seconds after he settled into the passenger's seat, Max fired off the first question.

"How was your flight?"

"Laborious."

"Don't you just love that stupid question?" she smiled. Before giving him an opportunity to respond, she asked a more important and less mundane request. "Do you have your credentials?"

"You're speaking to Field Agent Andrew Smyth?"

"Field Agent. You could have gone a little higher in the ranks."

"Considering I'm committing a felony crime, I thought I'd keep a low profile."

"Sam, no sweat! You'll be in and out in no time. Trust me, the rent-a-cop is clueless. But you need to find out why the Feds shut down the apiary."

He was not particularly thrilled with his assignment, but he was the one who showed up on her doorstep ready to offer his services. "Where was the body found?" he asked, stepping up to the plate.

"Inside his laboratory. It's located in the converted garage. The beekeeper's wife ran the office from within the main house, so she was not nearby at the time."

Max glanced at Sam, curious as to why the location of the body would be important. From his expression, he had already anticipated her question, but he did not give a hint as to his speculation.

"It's a place to start. How much farther?" he asked, eager to complete the mission, even before he got started.

"A few more minutes." Max used the time to throw another curve ball. "Hey, last night I was going through the beekeeper's calendar. Jeff visited him the week before leaving for Brazil. And there was this guy named Sorenson who showed up at the apiary numerous times. It could be our Norwegian, the one that Jeff met in Brazil. And get this. Remember that doctor from Japan? He visited the apiary the day after Jeff."

"Incredible."

"There are a lot of other names, but I need more time to sort through them." Max spotted the turnoff up ahead. "Okay, time to switch drivers." She pulled over to the side of the road. "It's right up there. Drive up that dirt road and just over the hill, you'll see the gate. There must be a surveillance camera, which is how the rent-a-cop caught me playing Poirot. And it was about this time yesterday that I was here, so you'll most likely run into the dear fellow—now, ready to do your magic?"

"Where are you going to be?"

"I'll hide in the back seat. Here, you take over." Max's agile body climbed into the back seat and ducked out of sight.

Sam shifted over into the driver's seat and groaned, "I can't believe you talked me into this." He lightly stepped on the gas pedal and eased the car along the dirt road until he met up with the gate fitting Max's description. With Max hidden from view, he got out of the car and perused the perimeter. It only took a few minutes before he heard the anticipated gruff voice barking orders.

"Hey, mister!" said the pudgy guard peering through the metal links. "You got no bidness snoopin' round. Now git, ya' hear?"

Sam flashed his badge in an authoritative manner, relishing the moment.

"Oh, sorry, Agent. May I ask what bidness you got?"

What a sucker! Max was right. Sam laid it on thick. "The bureau sent me back to check the place out. A double-check to make sure we missed nothing. It shouldn't take me too long."

"Well, c'mon in, but I'd appreciate it if you'd make it quick. My shift is bout ready to end." The would-be cop, with a bark worse that his bite, unlocked the gate and let Sam inside relocking the gate behind them.

Max, who had been listening in on the conversation, waited until she heard their footsteps move away. Alone at last, she unwound from her contorted position and peered through the window. She watched as Sam and the guard entered the makeshift base of operation. A half-hour later, Sam exited the building with the guard in tow. They appeared to be yucking it up, while Max returned to her crouched position in the backseat and waited for Sam to get back into the car.

With the sound of the guard relocking the gate, Max whispered, "What did you find out?" Almost as soon as she uttered the question, sirens began wailing off in the distance. Then the ominous sounds became progressively louder.

"Let's get out of here." Sam jammed his foot on the gas pedal.

"Take the first right up ahead," Max instructed as she slithered back into the front passenger's seat. "So tell me, what did you find out?"

"The Feds did their usual exemplary job of raiding the place. They must have taken truckloads of stuff out of there, including the bees. Not a hive in sight. Also, the hard drive was missing from the computer."

"Not a problem."

"What do you mean?"

"The beekeeper instructed his wife on how to scrub the drive should anything happen to him."

"Sounds as though he was expecting foul play."

"Sam, what is it?"

Max noticed that each time he looked in the rearview mirror he pressed harder on the gas pedal.

"The sirens we heard—just pulled into Clovis Hill."

Max turned around to look. She spotted two black sedans pulling into the driveway of the apiary. The guard was running back toward the gate. "What do you think that's all about?"

"I can only guess the Feds had the place bugged."

"And they saw you?"

Sam gave her a knowing stare and then refocused on the road.

"Dammit! Quick, take the next left. I need two minutes at the hotel to grab my things and checkout."

"I second that. Then let's get the hell out of Dodge."

"The hotel is only ten minutes from the Texas border."

"That puts the nearest airport in Lubbock. My guess is we're an hour and a half away. We'll catch a flight from there." Sam saw the sign for the Super 8 and swerved into the parking lot.

"I'll be right back." Max dashed out of the car and headed to her room.

Sam remained vigilant.

It was a fast shot across the border, as they now headed for Lubbock Preston Smith International Airport.

"What are you doing?" Sam asked.

Max was tapping wildly on her phone. "I'm canceling our flights out of Clovis and rebooking us on another flight. Looks like we can make the six-fifteen, stopping in Dallas. But we won't arrive until ten past midnight."

"I don't care what time; just get us out of here. But hold off on canceling our flights out of Clovis. If the Feds are on to us, let them think we're still around…" Sam's sentence appeared not to have ended.

"What are you thinking?" Max caught the hesitation.

"It's not what I'm thinking; it's what I'm feeling. And I have a really bad feeling about this case," he admitted.

Max reared her own frustration. "What is it they don't want us to know?! That's what haunts me."

"Aside from the fact that someone killed a beekeeper and a U.S. senator with bee venom, both of whom were four thousand miles apart from each other—your guess is as good as mine." Sam realized how bizarre his account of the situation sounded. And he sensed it was going to become even more inexplicable.

"We know that Oliver Prince was killed on December eighth, the same day Jeff left for Brazil. Manaus is two hours ahead of Clovis and Jeff was killed two days after he arrived."

"So, it's possible Prince could have told the killer that Jeff was in Brazil," Sam surmised. "Given the timeline, it's even possible that whomever murdered the beekeeper, also had the opportunity to get to Brazil and murder Jeff. You must admit, at least for doing in the beekeeper, it was the perfect murder."

"But why kill Jeff using the same method?"

"There's got to be more to it. Beekeepers breed bees and make honey, right?" Sam asked.

"At least that's what they were doing at Clovis Hill."

"Then why grow plants?"

"What?"

"The laboratory looked like a cannabis lab. There were three rows of tables, roughly ten feet long by four feet wide. The kind used for a raised garden bed. Above the tables hung an LED-based lighting system. The ones designed for commercial cultivation."

"You mean bioengineered to provide high levels of photosynthetically active radiation."

"Okay, smarty pants. But like the bees—all the plants were removed." Sam reached into his pocket and pulled out a few leaves and handed them to Max.

"Nice going! But what do you think they're all about?"

"I don't have a clue, but let's have the leaves analyzed as soon as we get back to DC."

"So, no bees. No papers. No plants. No beekeeper. At that point, why shut the place down? You know Sam, that was also the Princes' home." Max thought back to Miss Ellie and wondered how she was coping.

"It seemed rather extreme. I can only gather the Feds haven't finished looking. Looking for *what* is the question."

Chapter 19

The Consortium's Goal

"You damn fool! You've jeopardized the whole operation!"

Solum heard the fury in Slater's voice and took the offensive. "I got the beekeeper's data, just like you paid me for. And I took care of the senator and destroyed the package, as we agreed."

"Your choice of using venom for both the senator and Prince was stupid!"

Slater, adding insult after insult, moved Solum into a full-frontal assault. "As far as the senator was concerned, there was no plan to kill him, only to steal the package! But the poor bastard just walked in at the wrong time. As luck would have it, I still had the vials of venom left over from the beekeeper. So, I used one on him! What choice did I have? And what's the big deal anyway? Besides, I made it look like a lovefest gone bad." Solum smirked remembering the scene. Then his ire spewed. "For Christ sakes, who's going to link a senator's death in Brazil with a beekeeper in New Mexico."

Slater was beyond outrage. "I can name one possibility—Max Ford!"

At the sound of the name, Solum reeled in his fury and tried to maintain his cool. He asked, "How is she involved?"

"You killed one of her best friends!—and it wasn't the beekeeper. Now she's sniffing around Clovis with her new sidekick. And as far as the data we wanted, nada. There was nothing on the USB drive."

"What?! I copied it myself!" Even though he was still being chastised, Solum was glad for the diversion.

"He must have scrubbed the drive before you got there. Idiot!"

"You want me to go back in? He might have stashed the physical data somewhere in the facility."

"Our guys are handling it. For now, stand by. You'll be given one more chance."

The line went dead.

Solum did not like the use of the words *one more* or the idea of tangling with the director's henchman. A grave mistake Erog made when he hired Henry Little, the notorious assassin known as L to take out Max and some scientist she was protecting on an earlier case. L failed and never got another chance to make amends because Solum was ordered to take L out. And then he was sent to take out the scientist and anyone else who got in the way. Now, he had an uneasy feeling that Max was about to become his next target—again. *Why can't she stay out of the damn way?*

Slater pulled out his other phone, the one with the secure line and hit a button, the only button designed to work.

"Director, Prince has been taken care of, but unfortunately there were no data to retrieve. The hard drive was scrubbed before the beekeeper met his fate. The senator, however, was an unplanned casualty, but the package has been destroyed."

"So, this brings an end to this nonsense?"

"Not exactly. Max Ford showed up in Clovis, along with her new associate, Casper." Slater gritted his teeth and prepared himself for the onslaught.

"Every time she starts sniffing around, she puts all of our work in jeopardy! If we are to effect global governance, America's role must not fail! We cannot rely on a jungle of states to conform when they are each being shaped by their own citizens and being influenced by external geopolitical forces. And let's not forget the media. Fake or otherwise, it works against us when we are not fully controlling the message. None of this helps move us closer to a universal social contract. The only way to ensure that our planet is habitable for billions of people is to control Earth's precious resources necessary to sustain life. This can only happen through our efforts and our efforts alone. We must obtain absolute power over a New World Order!"

Slater had heard the speech before, but thought the director sounded a bit more morally desperate and treaded lightly. "How would you like me to handle the situation?"

"I keep you around to solve problems. You figure it out! Just take care of them!—Now!" The director did not restrain any signs of fury as Slater had hoped.

He took that to be a directive with zero wiggle room. "Yes, Director."

The call was ended.

Chapter 20

Good Grief

"Let's be seated," the counselor urged.

Chair legs scuffed across the floor as they were being placed in the form of a circle. Quickly, they were filled with ten lost souls.

"Let's pray."

In unison, they uttered: "God grant me the serenity to accept the things I cannot change, courage to change the things I can, and wisdom to know the difference." They were words from the Serenity Prayer, which they had recited many times before.

"Welcome. It's good to see a few familiar faces and a few new ones. For those who missed last week's session, we discussed grief and how it affects your relationships. Would anyone like to share the takeaway?" The counselor waited for a volunteer.

A hand went up in the air.

"Yes, Allison."

"Grief is an individual experience. No one can grieve for me. Friends think they're helping by telling me that they understand how I feel, but they have no idea. The heartache is so personal. I admit I don't even know how my children are grieving."

"You need to find ways to express your feelings and not keep them bottled up inside," the counselor stated, coaxing her to continue.

"It's easier to talk about how I'm feeling in this group, knowing that others in this room have also experienced a form of grief." Allison scanned the group and kidded, "As long as no one tries to make me feel better." They chuckled as she continued. "I have learned that if we listen but not judge, it starts the healing process. I am trying to do that with my children."

"Well said, Allison. Would anyone else care to share their thoughts?"

Another hand shot up.

"You're new to our group. Please tell us your name?" the counselor asked.

"Samantha."

"Welcome, Samantha," the group greeted her.

"How do you grieve?" she asked. "For me it would be a blessing, but I'm stuck in anger."

"You are grieving. But you're using your anger to avoid the pain. Understand anger is okay. A colleague of mine, Andy Davidson, explained it best: 'You need to recognize you're not yourself, then express your anger, and then ask for forgiveness. That will bring you the most relief. By asking for and granting relief you will eventually be able to let the anger go.'"

"I'm so pissed all the time," Samantha admitted.

"Embrace it! Once you accept that it's normal to feel resentful, you'll get through the anger. But understand the pain may never totally go away. You will, however, learn to find a way for peace and the pain to coexist. Let's review the phases of grief, for those of you who were not here last week."

The counselor walked over to the easel and flipped back to the sheet listing the five phases. Written in large lettering was:

Impact

Chaos

Adapting

Equilibrium

Transformation

One of the newcomers asked, "I thought the stages of grief were denial, anger, bargaining, depression, and acceptance?"

"You're referring to the stages defined by Elizabeth Kübler-Ross, a Swiss psychiatrist, as detailed in her book *On Death and Dying*. But the ones listed on the flipboard are outlined by Joanne Jozefowski in her book, *The Phoenix Phenomenon: Rising from the Ashes of Grief*. I personally don't believe everyone follows the same pattern of grief, in the same way I've disagreed with Gail Sheehy's *Passages*. Humans react differently based on their own environment and experiences. I find Jozefowski's approach more helpful and positive for one trying to rebuild a shattered life."

"In what way?" Allison asked, hoping her own personal tragedy could be put to rest.

"Instead of working through the grief stage by stage, as Kubler-Ross outlines, Jozefowski provides guidelines. Her book discusses 'how to avoid hazards, adapt with healthy coping mechanisms, and eliminate unnecessary suffering.'"

Allison wanted to understand. "So, until you accept the impact of a tragedy, whether it's coping with denial or fear, and you manage to wade through all the chaos, it's not until then that you can begin to adapt?" she stated, looking for confirmation.

"In some form," the counselor replied. "There are those who may skip over the chaos completely. Micro-managing one's life could be a very positive coping mechanism. Most important, you will begin putting your life back in order and engage once again with loved ones. But it's imperative to learn to accept their help. Jozefowski says it's important to 'take control of grieving so that grief does not control you,' then you can 'slowly accept the new reality.'"

The counselor continued to walk through the other phases on the list, addressing questions along the way, until she sensed the group was reflecting on the chaos in their own lives and were looking for ways to negotiate a better existence. She also thought it a fitting end to the session. "Please help yourself to coffee and cookies in the back of the room. But first, remember, incredible changes will happen in your life, but only when you decide to take control. Just don't spend time dwelling on the things you can't control."

The same chair legs scuffed across the floor in the opposite direction as they were being placed along the perimeter of the room. Then, the ten souls, seeming less lost, headed for refreshments.

"You don't talk much, do you?" Allison asked.

The gentleman standing next to her reached over to fill his coffee cup. He was the same man who sat across from her each week. "My name is Steven."

"Hi, Steven. I'm Allison." She tapped her coffee to his in a symbolic toast. "You've been coming to this group for a couple of weeks, but you've yet to have spoken."

"I find it more cathartic to listen to others grieving."

"Did you lose your wife?"

"No, Sister."

Allison continued to rattle on in a nervous tenor, surprised that she found Steven to be quite charming, in a mysterious sort of way. And as much as she would have liked to continue the conversation, she needed to get home to the kids. "I have to go, but I hope to see you next week."

"Perhaps. Drive carefully, Allison." Steven was the first to leave.

Chapter 21
Sleepless Inside The Beltway

Max gave up the fight, unable to sleep, and moseyed into the kitchen to grab a cup of coffee. She spent the remaining predawn hours trying to identify the mysterious plant leaves Sam found at the Clovis Hill Apiary. She had her suspicions, but needed confirmation before proceeding in the wrong direction.

After painstakingly using various Apps, she was getting nowhere. The PlantNet Plant Identification, Plantifier, and the Virginia Tech Tree ID Apps, came up short.

Who do I think I am, a botanist? "Aha, a botanist, of course!"

Without delay, she scanned a photo of one of the leaves to a professor she met earlier at Virginia Polytechnic Institute in Blacksburg, Virginia. With her fingers crossed, she hoped the professor would go straight to the source; the one who created the Virginia Tech Tree ID App. Once the email and photo were on their way, she grabbed another dose of caffeine and began to tackle the beekeeper's calendar with more vigorous scrutiny. While she scribbled a handful of notes, she made a few surprising discoveries.

Slater had two appointments with Oliver Prince—February 20 and November 27. *Something about that last date seems oddly familiar.* Max skimmed the other notes she had previously taken while reviewing Jeff's calendar. "Hold on a sec! Mizukami—it has to be a coincidence." The dates lined up. It was the day after Jeff visited the apiary and ten days before Prince was killed. *Japan is not exactly around the corner,* she thought.

Justin Slater had stooped to new subterranean levels, along with his highly questionable methods. But there was one question that begged further investigation: *how did Slater make the connection between Jeff, the beekeeper, and a doctor from Japan?*

Her mind suddenly shifted to the plant leaf and then to Sam. "Where the hell is he?" she said aloud in a mildly annoyed tone. She was eager to share the information she had uncovered. All of a sudden, she found it a nuisance not to have him under the same roof and readily available—even though the rented apartment he latched onto was only a few blocks away. Now edging toward the noon hour, she had yet to lay eyes on him.

Reeling in her impatience, Max switched her focus and began hoping for something concrete from Virginia Tech, as she moved on to the next mystery. "Now, who's Sorenson?" Miss Ellie did not recall his first name, but the last name appeared three times on the calendar. What puzzled Max was Sorenson's few scheduled appointments that were scattered over the calendar year. But Miss Ellie said he was a frequent visitor. Without a full name other than he worked for the FDA, and that he most likely met Jeff in Brazil, it was akin to looking for the identity of a plant leaf. "Another strikeout!" While sulking on the proverbial bench, the phone rang. "Or maybe not," she said, as she noticed the caller ID.

"Hello, this is Max Ford."

"This is Professor Cleveland from the Department of Biological Sciences at Virginia Tech. I received a photo of a plant leaf that I understand you'd like to know its identity."

"Thank you for calling, Professor. Were you able to identify it?" She refrained from sounding overly eager.

"May I ask where you got the leaf?" The professor asked. His curiosity was obvious.

"It was discovered during an investigation. Please tell me what you can about the origin."

"The name is *Baccharis dracunculifolia*."

Max was flabbergasted, but elated that her suspicion was confirmed.

"It's a rare plant used for medicinal purposes and comes from South America. It's used to produce green..."

"Propolis!" she blurted out.

"Impressive. Now that you know what the plant is, are you aware that it's listed on the FDA's Poisonous Plant Database? Unfortunately, there's no GRIN number."

"A what number?"

"The Germplasm Resources Information Network established by the USDA. It provides information on the genetic material in plants and animals."

"It doesn't make sense that the FDA would consider it poisonous, if there's no record of it in the information network."

"Yes, I found that rather odd myself. I hope at least knowing the species is of help."

"Thank you, Professor; it's most helpful."

"Good day, then."

As Max heard the click on the other line, she mulled over her East-Meets-West theory. *Could Dr. Mizukami have been helping Prince develop a super pill? Beekeeper becomes chemist? Instead of importing the drug illegally, perhaps someone or some entity had him making it illegally under the radar?*

"You must be enchanted by the sound of your voice."

Max did not hear Sam arrive and was obviously surprised, but it didn't stop her from catching his comment and volleyed with a quick retort. "Taking the morning off to decorate?"

Sam ignored her. "I see you've been burning the midnight oil as well." It was clear from the tousled mess of hair and the bloodshot eyes that she had spent little time in her apartment upstairs.

"You, too, huh?"

"You might say I've been putting in a little overtime on this case myself. And now, I may have a theory. Give me ten and then pop into my office."

"First, how about I order in pizza? I'm starved."

"Great, me too. By the way, have you noticed that black Mercedes parked out front? It was there the day you left for Clovis and it's there again today."

Max got up from her chair and walked out into the reception area and over to the window. "I think I saw the car once when I was out for my morning run." Max got a cold tingle up her spine, but blew it off. "He's probably just a driver for one of the neighbors waiting for a pickup. We do have several illustrious government officials living in the hood. Aside from yourself, of course."

"Max, look at the street. It's empty. So why is he parked out front?" Sam asked.

They momentarily locked eyes, sharing the same thought.

"I'm not going to live in fear. Let me go order the pizza and then I have something to tell you too."

Sam was concerned that she did not take the stranger seriously. But he remained seated on the sofa, keeping a watchful eye on the car.

Chapter 22

Pizza Delivery

"Dimitri's Pizzeria."

"Goodness gracious, I got the man himself."

"Hey, Max, what can I get ya?"

"The usual—wait a minute, make that two. One medium, one small."

"The same?"

"Yes, and can you get them to me in the next ten minutes?"

"Sure, thing! It must be your lucky day; I put a similar order in the oven a few minutes ago."

"You're the best—and Dimitri, I need another favor."

"Anything for you, doll!"

"Can you have Gianni deliver the small pizza first, to the guy in the black Mercedes parked across the street in front of my house."

"Aren't you a sweetheart."

"In ten."

"He'll be there."

Max returned to the reception area and sat down next to Sam. "Hey, guess what this is?" she asked, dangling one of the plant leaves, distracting him from the scene outside.

"Seriously?"

"*Baccharis dracunculifolia.*"

"You took the words right out of my mouth."

"Ha ha. Now we know the name of this monster. Get this: it's listed as a poisonous plant on the FDA's database."

"Hey, that's the same plant the Japanese doctor was using to cure people!"

"Correctamundo! And that doctor met with our beekeeper. Incidentally, the same day Slater showed up at the apiary."

Sam raised an eyebrow; it finally hit him. "Wait a minute. The Japanese doc produced propolis from that plant?"

"Terrific memory. So perhaps Prince was learning how to do the same thing."

"Max, Prince was a beekeeper; he'd have access to all the propolis he needed."

"But not as powerful."

"Well, I have my own theory."

"Hold that thought; here comes the pizza."

Sam saw the delivery guy park his bicycle in front of the Victorian. "What's he doing?"

The kid was heading over toward the Mercedes.

"Wait a minute. You'll see." Max flashed him a wink.

They watched as the driver slowly rolled down the window, but the face of the driver was obscured by the pizza box. But for a split second, when Gianni stepped away, Max caught a glimpse causing her to grab her chest. *It's not possible.* She tried to hide any further reaction even though the virtual punch to the solar plexus made it awkward to breathe.

Sam could not help but notice the color drain from her face. "Max, are you okay?"

Without responding, she jumped up and went over to open the front door.

"Hey, Max." Gianni handed her the large pizza, and the receipt folded in half—something he had never done before. Usually, it was taped to the top of the box.

"The guy said thanks." Gianni flashed a smile.

As soon as Max handed him his tip, he turned and bounded back down the steps, calling out "Thank you!" Then, he hopped back on his bicycle and sped away.

"Let me take this into the kitchen," she said as she breezed by. When out of eyesight, she clutched her chest again. Once she was able to expel the pent-up air in her lungs, she unfolded the receipt. Seconds later, she hustled into her office and grabbed her coat and bag. "Sam, there's something I forgot to take care of," she called out. "I won't be long."

"I thought you were hungry? And what's with the other pizza?"

Her movements were so swift, his questions barely touched her ears as she passed by him again and walked out the front door without responding.

Sam looked back out the window and watched Max descend the steps to the sidewalk. Then he looked across the street—the car was gone. Suddenly, his apprehension about the case was growing; it did not help that Max's behavior was becoming more erratic. But while his concern lingered, the smell of pepperoni pizza wafted from the kitchen, replacing his immediate worry. *Maybe she just had to run an errand like she said,* he thought.

Chapter 23

Not A Walk In The Park

Max pulled out the receipt from her coat pocket and read the note again: **Meet me in the park — you know where.** *It can't be him. Why did he come back?* An eerie sensation festered inside her, but it only fed her voracious curiosity. She walked down the sidewalk with calculated steps and hovered near the buildings, careful to stay out of Sam's eyeshot, should he still be leering out the window. Then, when she thought the coast was clear, she crossed the street and walked into Lincoln Park. As she wended her way toward the park bench, the same bench where Senator Sherman Spark's corpse had lain months earlier, she questioned, *And why this spot?* The location of her first case. She also hoped this was a sick joke and that her eyes had deceived her. *The driver inside the black Mercedes can't be Daniel.* As she approached, she saw a man seated on the bench, with his back toward her. She clutched her bag tighter against her side and felt the outline of the Sig Sauer.

When he heard her footsteps, he turned slightly in her direction.

"Jesus Christ—it's really you."

"Hello, Claudia."

"Don't call me that!—she's dead!" Max shook her head trying to rid the vision of Daniel seated before her; it was to no avail. "What are you doing here?"

"Maybe to make amends. Hey, sis, I was only doing my job. All you had to do was surrender the USB drive, the one with the scientists' revelations."

"But why kill Noble?"

"He was true to his name. Sure, he aligned with our mission and converted to what the Consortium was trying to accomplish. But he also understood to what extent we would go to protect the director. In essence, he knew too much; he had to go. And besides— he was going to kill you, dear sister."

"And now you've come to kill me? This is a surrealistic nightmare."

"It doesn't have to be. You can walk away." Daniel remained silent and continued to stare, marveling at how his younger sister had developed into a beautiful, and extremely formidable, woman— so formidable that the Consortium considered her a major threat.

For some unforeseen reason, Max started to let go of her anger briefly, as she remembered her older brother in earlier times. Until flashbacks of that horrible night reappeared. Daniel and her father arguing. The sound of a gunshot. Her father lying dead. Bombarded with visions, she overlooked the significance of the bench and sat next to him.

"The Consortium killed our father—and now you kill for them," she stated with unexpected calm. "Daniel, what happened to you?" She desperately wanted to understand.

"You got lucky, kid. They threw you into foster care. For me, the CIA decided I'd be more viable as a trained assassin. But one day I had an epiphany and went rogue. Years later, the Consortium recruited me. So, I guess you could say my fate changed." Daniel smirked.

"You still kill people." The sense of unease returned.

"But now it's for a just cause. The members of the Consortium comprise many of the world's richest and most powerful people, who believe they will better serve humanity for the next millennia."

"I fail to see how killing is just! Whatever your lofty motives."

"We recognize the inefficiency of the world's governments when dealing with society's most urgent issues. We've lost faith in those governments. And having both the means and the motivation to seize the power, the Consortium took it into their own hands to advance our cause."

"Under whose authority?"

"Whose authority? God's! If we don't protect our world resources and control our exploding population, our future will be bleak. Billions of people will be born into poverty. We'll murder each other in a war for water, food and oil! Controlling the world's population by allocating resources is our only hope."

"So, their answer is to murder in advance those who threaten this so-called utopia, which they believe they're building?" Max's grave doubts resonated.

"We're talking about the survival of humanity. In that context, none of us individually are more important than the mission. Noble missed that fine point."

"Christ, Daniel! All these years, I thought you might have killed Dad, only to learn that you work for the same people who murdered him."

"It's a rather sardonic twist that destiny handed us."

"So now what?"

Daniel changed his tone again, this time remembering his purpose. "We are sitting on this park bench to remind you how close you came to be being killed again. L may have screwed up, but as you can see for yourself, there is an endless supply of assassins where he came from. And now you're getting yourself into a whole heap of new trouble."

Max had a sudden flashback of Jax in the alley behind The Bachelor's Mill, standing over the body of the deadly assassin L. She suddenly felt ashamed that she ever considered Jax a suspect. Her ire returned. "How the hell do you know..."

Daniel cut her off. "Your luck will run out if you don't back off this case." He pulled the brim of his cap down farther on his forehead and placed his hands in his pockets. He looked straight ahead. It was obvious he had no intention of giving her an answer.

"That sounds like a threat." *But could Daniel have killed L to save my life? Did he kill Noble to save me as well?* Even with her lingering thoughts, she knew she would pry nothing more out of him for the moment. She would have to wait for another encounter. "How do I get in touch with you?"

"You don't. I'll contact you. But in what terms is in your hands." Daniel leaned over to give her an unexpected kiss on the cheek. Then stood up and walked away.

Max shuddered as she watched him disappear from the gravel path. The vision of Miss Ellie running her finger along the side of her cheek entered her mind, leaving her momentarily paralyzed. Then in a baffling moment, the sun peeked through the trees for a split second, long enough to illuminate the left side of Daniel's face. "Oh, thank God; there's no scar." She was relieved and thankful for the quick flash of light.

Chapter 24
The Whiteboard Conclusions

Sam heard Max turn the front doorknob and skirted into the reception area. "What's with the swift retreat, my dear? And by the by, who was that guy?" Sam had a vivid image of the look on her face when she caught a glimpse of the mystery man.

"How poetic—and I have no idea who it was. The pizza box was in the way. All I saw was a guy that looked like Chef Boyardee etched on top of the box." She shrugged her shoulders. "Gianni said the guy thanked him for the pizza and took off." *If I tell him Daniel's back, he'll move into overprotection hyper-mode and get in the way.* Max held off for the moment.

"Same here, couldn't see a thing." *Hmm,* Sam wondered, doubting her every word. He also knew any attempt to drag it out of her would be fruitless. *On second thought.* "Where did you take off to in such a hurry?" He gave it a shot.

She ignored the question and stared out the front window.

"Max, what's with you? I saw the look on your face when that guy rolled down the window. You looked as though you saw a ghost."

"Please, Sam. Chalk it up to this case and a lack of sleep."

He relented for the time being. "Go heat up a slice a pizza and c'mon into my office."

"In a minute." Max needed time to wrap her head around what had just happened. She headed into her own office and tried to pull it together. Once less flustered, she joined Sam.

"Wow! What are you working on now—missing-persons cases?" Max asked, seeming more like herself. Plastered in front of her, Sam had projected seventy-seven headshots from his computer onto the wall—seven rows down with eleven rows across.

Pleased at the sudden change in her demeanor, he responded, "No, sorry to say they're dead doctors. Remember Erin Elizabeth?"

Max was aghast at first by the sheer number of faces. Then she recalled the *Health Nut News* site. "Oh, yeah, I vaguely remember seeing that posted on her website."

"On the far left, fourth row down, is Dr. Bradstreet's photo, the first doctor Erin reported dead."

"Wait a minute—Jeff's last words to Allison had to do with Bradstreet. Something about needing to ensure it would never happen again."

"Well, evidently something happened. I worked through the night trying to connect your notorious dancing dots."

"You have a theory?"

"Sort of. Whenever a doctor died, Erin reported the death on her site."

Max again studied the wall trying to assess the magnitude. "Seventy-seven doctors met their deaths. That doesn't compute as a coincidence."

"As of now, Erin has reported over eighty deaths, and most practitioners were associated with alternative or Eastern medicine in some capacity. From the evidence, many of these deaths can without a doubt be explained—but just as many are suspicious."

"What's in it for Erin? What's her end game?"

"I can't speak to her intent, but she's created quite a conspiracy theory. From the perspective of this case, it all appears to start and end with Dr. Jeffrey Bradstreet!"

"Allison's conversation with Jeff seemed to suggest that…" Max's voice trailed off as she stared at the wall.

"Max, are you with me?" Sam studied her face.

"Yes—I'm listening. You reported earlier that Bradstreet was illegally using GcMAF treatments to reverse autism. And that the Feds raided his office, days before his death. But how does this connect to Jeff and the beekeeper?"

"Hear me out. Bradstreet's body was discovered on June 19, 2015. It appeared that he committed suicide by shooting himself in the chest."

"Still seems like an odd way to kill yourself," Max interjected.

"My thought as well. But then two days later, on June twenty-first, incidentally on Father's Day, Baron Holt, a chiropractor, was found dead while visiting Jacksonville, Florida. But he lived in North Carolina, near where Bradstreet's body was located. Reports indicated he was there to have his spine realigned, but according to Erin's sources, Holt, a devout Christian, died from an overdose of a street drug called 'Molly'—leaving a wife and a three-year-old daughter behind. On the same day, another chiropractor by the name of Bruce Hedendal was found dead in his car after a sporting event. Some attribute it to heat exhaustion; others find it suspicious. Then again, on June twenty-ninth, Dr. Teresa Sievers, who practiced holistic medicine, was discovered bludgeoned to death in her home in Bonita Springs. But this case was a weird one. Apparently, the husband is accused of hiring a boyhood friend, who was then joined by another friend to do the dirty deed, supposedly for the insurance money. The boyhood friend pleaded guilty to murder and was convicted. But as of May, two years later, both the husband and the other accomplice were still on trial facing the death penalty. And given all the evidence, some are still convinced the husband was framed. What's most intriguing is that the local news reached out to the FDA in an attempt to link Sievers's murder to the Bradstreet case and they were pushed off to the Georgia State Attorney's Office. Again, according to Erin, the Georgia official involved in the Bradstreet case declined to comment on whether there was a possible criminal investigation underway." Sam could see that Max was becoming impatient and quickly rattled off the next depressing story. "The same day Sievers was murdered, Dr. Jeffrey Whiteside, a pulmonologist, walked away from a family vacation in Wisconsin, reportedly after an argument with his wife. Three weeks later, the body turned up, along with a .22 caliber gun that had been purchased back in the '60s by his father. The death, like Bradstreet's, was deemed a suicide."

"Sorry, but it seems to be a wide stretch between *your* infamous dots."

"Agreed, but in the span of ten days, five doctors are dead. One presumed of natural causes, one murder, and three suicides—yet all are painted with the same suspicious brush."

"Is that Erin's opinion or the plain facts?"

"Not sure, but it could be a motive."

"Sam, I agree it doesn't smell right, but doctors die just like the rest of us. There are over a million doctors in the US alone. I read a stat somewhere, that given the ratio of doctors to the general population who die each year, upward of seven hundred doctors a month could expect to die from some accidental or natural cause."

"Granted, some of these doctor's deaths could be explained away, but let me highlight a few more that have gone unanswered. Starting with Dr. Nicholas Gonzales, who died a month after Bradstreet's body was uncovered. He was considered one of the preeminent authorities on curing pancreatic cancer. He advocated a protocol using detoxification, diet, and supplements, including pancreatic enzymes."

"Hold on a sec." Max brought up the message app on her phone and looked for Allison's text message, the one with the list of alternative doctors Jeff had contacted. She looked up at Sam. "Einstein, you just might be on to something. Gonzales was one of the doctors Jeff contacted in early 2015 when he was first searching for a cure. The protocol you mentioned was the same one Allison described to me and Jeff followed." Max's interest was suddenly heightened. "What was his cause of death?"

"At first, it was reported that he died of a heart attack, but a preliminary autopsy found the results to be inconclusive. I couldn't find any mention of the outcome anywhere. However, suspicions continue to swirl to this day, with some even claiming that succinylcholine, a neuromuscular paralytic drug, was injected to mimic a heart attack."

"Aha, the old CIA frozen-dart theory."

"It may not be that crazy. Gonzales wrote a book called *What Went Wrong*, where he exposed the sabotage of clinical trials conducted to compare his protocol against the chemotherapeutic drug called gemcitabine, which goes by the brand name Gemzar. It's used in the treatment of pancreatic cancer. He blamed the poor trial design and implementation, along with the mismanagement of two government oversight offices and their scientists. He alleged the results were manipulated to yield a negative conclusion. He went so far as to acknowledge that he was forced to use unconscious patients, who were obviously unable to swallow the almost 200 pills per day, as part of his cancer protocol. Gonzales was also heard saying on numerous occasions that 'he thought Big PhRMA wanted him to get hit by a bus or that he might die suddenly.'"

"Are you suggesting that Jeff's quest for a cure may have by accident tossed him into the middle of a major cover-up?"

"Let's come back to that question. Listen to the woes of two more doctors and then see what you conclude. A well-respected oncologist from New York, by the name of Mitch Gaynor, and a huge proponent of alternative medicine, died on September sixteenth in the same year."

"And how did he die?" Max was quick to ask.

"Suicide."

"What's that make—five, six alleged suicides?" She was clearly baffled.

"I've lost count, but I fear we've only scratched the surface. But this case in particular is a real spy thriller. Four days before his death, Gaynor was interviewed on *The Big Picture* by Thom Hartmann on the Russian RT news network. He was promoting his new book *Gene Therapy Plan*, which had been published a few months earlier. And according to Erin, he had sent a copy of his book to her around the same time."

"So, his life was moving in the right direction..."

Sam noticed Max was about to expound and held up his hand to hold her off. "In November, the founder of RT, Mikhail Lesin, was beaten to death in his hotel room in Washington, DC. It was the night before he was scheduled to meet with someone at the Department of Justice. Rumor had it that the *Fast and Furious* AG wanted to know how the Russian propaganda machine worked and believed Lesin was a good resource.

Max could not resist any longer. "Please, not Russian collusion again."

"Hey, Miss Sharpshooter, please don't shoot the messenger. One more. In January 2016, Dr. John Marshall..."

"Sam, I get it!" Max's mind was spinning like a top with the number of deaths occurring in a comparatively short time span. At the same time, she was developing her own conspiracy theory. It began to mimic Erin Elizabeth's. Then, the immortal words of Joe Friday popped into her head. *Just the facts, ma'am.*

"I know this seems unbelievable, but hear this one out." Sam gave her a moment to refocus and then continued. "As I was saying, Dr. Marshall, a surgeon at the Mann-Grandstaff Veterans Affairs Medical Center in Washington State, was found dead in the Spokane River the day after he went out for a morning run, never to return home. After an investigation, the Spokane Police Department reported it as an accidental drowning. But his wife, Suzanne Marshall, also a doctor, didn't buy it and hired Ted Pulver, a private detective. *The Spokesman-Review*, a local publication, reported that Pulver 'believes at least two people with military or police training grabbed Marshall, waterboarded him, killed him, and staged his body on the banks of the river in the early morning.' There was more evidence to support his assertion. To be transparent, there were reports of marital and financial difficulties, but that would not explain the contrary opinions between the police and private investigations. You have to admit, there may be more than meets the eye."

"Being in the biz, I agree," Max replied. "But you still have me hanging by the thumbs."

Although, a theory was crystalizing, a sudden flashback of her seated next to Daniel in the park and his threatening her to get off the case was unsettling.

"Sam, if doctors practicing alternative medicine are being killed—and in many instances their deaths are made to look like suicide, you—we—better be right!"

"What other conclusion is there to draw? "Sam asked.

"But what does this have to do with Jeff?" Max demanded.

"Remember, Jeff met with Dr. Stanislaw Burzysnki." Sam was growing impatient.

"Yes, but he's alive."

"Surprisingly, because Burzynski is on record as having questioned the billions of dollars at stake and to what lengths Big PhRMA would go in an effort to silence those promoting natural cures."

"Didn't he also say, 'that being a holistic health care provider that promotes natural health can now be dangerous to one's own health'?"

"Something like that. But his Personalized Gene-Targeted Cancer Therapy was also consistent with Dr. Gaynor's Gene Therapy—who is not alive, to make a point. But to answer your first question, I'm starting to think Jeff might have been trying to prove not only that these doctors are connected, but for the ones who met a tragic end—their deaths may be tied into the big picture."

Max pondered for a moment as her gut tried to steer her away from Sam's conclusion. "Maybe that's how it started. Or perhaps it goes back to the beginning and is somehow connected to one of his committee investigations."

"But?" Sam sensed there was more.

"But, after Jeff faced his own health crisis, he may have intentionally become part of a larger battle—fighting for alternative medicine. It would pull the curtain away and put a new spotlight on ways to treat cancer. Possibly even prove that Bradstreet, Gonzales, and Burzynski were all correct."

Sam refocused on the wall with the faces of victims looking back. "Many of the profiles you're looking at are medical doctors who replaced the traditional course of radiation and chemotherapy with alternative medicine. I agree some of these people were not doctors per se, but naturopaths. But they all led the pack, promoting diet and exercise as a means to treat diseases. I've been reading up on this stuff, and some of their cures are rather miraculous as shown in their case studies."

"Then it begs the question," she emphasized. "Why would anyone be resistant to anything that could cure autism, Alzheimer's, and a myriad of cancers?"

"Call me a cynic, but in the words of Woodward and Bernstein, *follow the money*. The cancer industry is more like an industrial complex. It includes radiation and chemotherapy drugs that produced over one hundred billion dollars in revenue last year. Their profits are predicted to increase eight percent each year going forward. Reportedly, share buybacks and increased dividends for the major drug companies overshadowed their research development by a significant margin. Drug development was being supplemented by decades-old patents, at a time when drug costs were skyrocketing. Straight and to the point, I don't see where there's a monetary incentive for Big PhRMA to want to find a cure. After all, who would willingly empty their wallet? Problem is, there's no way of proving it."

Sam had been carrying on for over an hour, listing the sad tales of doctors' deaths, reading at times from autopsy reports, other times from the *Health Nut News* site—but in the end, there was still no direct motive or link to Jeff's death. However, both he and Max conceded that somehow Big PhRMA was involved, even if only based on circumstantial inferences.

Throughout Sam's filibuster, Max had multitasked, jotting down a series of notes. She took a moment to study them again. Six of the names jumped off the note pad. "Hold on; I want to confirm something." Max scooted into her office and retrieved the beekeeper's calendar and returned within seconds.

"What is it this time?" Sam was hoping for a breakthrough.

"Give me a moment." Max skimmed down the list of appointments and tallied up the numbers in her head. Then she grabbed her phone and retrieved Allison's text message with the list of alternative medicine practitioner Jeff had contacted. "Unbelievable!"

"Max, cut with the suspense. What gives?"

"In the last two and a half years, Jeff contacted twenty-two of the doctors you mentioned—seventeen are dead. Sam! Eight died suspiciously—and they also met with our beekeeper. That must be the connection! One that explains why Jeff lost his life."

"What the frig is happening?" Sam sighed. Then he caught that look in her eye. "Max?"

"I can't shake this gnawing feeling. There's something we're missing."

"You mean separate from these deaths?"

"Hold that thought. You want a cup of coffee?"

"Sure thing, if you're buying!" He needed the pick-me-up because he wasn't processing. Either that or Max was more befuddled than he expected.

"I'll be right back." Max sauntered into the kitchen to fetch the java. It also gave her a few minutes to roll a few things around in that complex brain of hers. *How is Daniel, and by way of extension, the Consortium, wrapped up in this whole torrid mess? What threat could these practitioners possibly pose to the Consortium?*

Questions she could not yet bring to the discussion.

Chapter 25

Admissions and Denials

Max returned with two cups of much-needed caffeine hoping it would spur them onto a finite conclusion. She handed one cup to Sam, but remained standing, contemplating the faces of the dead doctors. As the faces peered back, there was one face that was wedged in her mind; the one that shared her own flesh and blood. *How can Daniel possibly be involved?*

Sam left her to ponder while trying to read her mind. Unsuccessful and unable to wait any longer, he asked, "And your conclusion is, Madame Investigator?"

"Okay, say we assume all roads lead to Big PhRMA and the FDA, its unwitting handmaiden. But with everything we've uncovered, I still find it farfetched that they are intentionally fighting natural remedies that have promising results. That would be absurd and inhuman. And you have to admit they do serve a purpose. The FDA protects us at some level from toxic foods and drugs. And Big PhRMA manufactures drugs that alleviate symptoms and sometime cure, as with antibiotics. So, we can't knock them completely."

"Max, are you getting soft? Look no further than your medicine cabinet. Have you seen Big PhRMA's advertising campaign lately? It's on steroids. They audaciously call it GoBoldly." Sam was suddenly distracted by her rapid movements, interrupting his chance to continue.

With a coffee cup in one hand and thumbing her phone with the other, Max did a quick search. "Listen to this," she said, "the GoBoldly website appears to provide an opportunity for the public, and I quote, 'explore the innovative research and technological breakthroughs of America's biopharmaceutical industry, and get to know the people behind the fight to prevent, treat, and cure disease'. It sounds proactive."

"Except for the fact that many in the public have already been brainwashed to believe that every time they face an ailment, there's a pill that can come to the rescue. Already, three-quarters of the population are over the age of fifty and are on prescription drugs, which makes it also highly profitable."

"You're so cynical."

"It's easy to be, Max, because what's damning is the FDA's history of painfully slow clinical trials and drug approvals for cancer treatments. And at the same time, the pharmaceutical companies continue to pump out drugs with cute names and happy-looking colors—all the while, knowing they only treat the symptoms, not the cure. The model is broken, hopefully not beyond repair, but while we're getting sicker, their wallets are getting fatter. It defies the imagination to think they're that naïve and unaware that they're creating a society becoming chronically dependent on these drugs. What does it take to see that the opioid epidemic is out of control?"

"Calm down or you're going to need one of those pills. You've made your point and perhaps you're right. Jeff was interested in all the possibilities alternative medicine had to offer. We know that from Allison. But why meet with Slater so often? I mean, based on your theory, he would be fighting against them."

"Slater also met with the beekeeper. The more logical conclusion would be that he was exuding pressure by using the FDA to go after the doctors to suppress their ideas."

"But why?" She looked at Sam curiously.

"Remember; you're the one who threw out the possibility that Dr. Mizukami was helping Prince develop a super pill."

"Right, and if our beekeeper was getting into a new line of work, then there must be powerful people providing the funding. The apiary was a relatively miniscule operation."

"And like Bradstreet, the beekeeper's death was also intertwined with the FDA. You can't deny that," Sam reminded her.

Max took a moment to consider what they were suggesting. "Let's slow down. I'm still grappling with the idea that Big PhRMA or the FDA would dirty their hands. Granted, in spite of their clean hands, the FDA has a tradition of raiding offices and shutting down practices for reasons of their own."

"And they turned a blind eye when companies repackaged orphan drugs or drugs that fell into disfavor for insufficient warnings of side effects and even worse, death."

"Orphan drugs?" That was a new one for Max.

"They're drugs that are developed to treat specific rare diseases. But then the drugs are relabeled, which is referred to as off-label and marketed for other uses. It's a tactic used by the pharmaceutical companies to generate huge profits before its patent expires and a generic drug hits the market."

"Isn't that rather unethical to transform an old pill into a new one? In name only?"

"Yes, but that doesn't stop them from chasing after more dollars. According to a *Wall Street Journal* article by Peter Loftus, 'Since 2013, the price of a 40-year-old, off-patent cancer drug in the US has risen 15-fold, putting the life-extending medicine out of reach for some patients.' An example of off-label, is when Eli Lilly took Prozac off the market due to reported incidents of suicide that had surfaced and attributed to the drug. So, what did they do?"

"Called it something else?" Max played along.

"Precisely. The same drug became Sarafem. It sounded less threatening and much more feminine to accommodate you ladies. It was then marketed to treat severe PMS rather than depression. You can also be sure it cost the consumer more. And there's more than enough evidence that Big PhRMA resorted to this 'disease-mongering' with a consistent habit for dressing up old pills, giving them new names to address the new societal anxieties that they themselves created. There's also an abundance of evidence that Big PhRMA owns the FDA, giving them complete autonomy and control. I remember reading a Harvard study that proved the allegation. Give me a minute to look it up for you."

Sam was on a roll and Max did not want to steal his thunder. She waited patiently as she sipped her coffee.

"Here it is. It was written by a group of Harvard professors, titled *Institutional Corruption of Pharmaceuticals and the Myth of Safe and Effective Drugs.* According to their report, ninety percent of all new drugs approved by the FDA over the last 30 years, have little or no advantages compared to the existing drugs. The report slams the administration for its failure to 'honestly and ethically approve new drugs.' It states that 'the FDA cannot be trusted.' They claim to produce solid evidence 'to show that the FDA is nothing more than a pay-for-play front group that caters strictly to the interests of the pharmaceutical industry.' So, there it is in black and white."

"You know that Lou Dobbs guy. Well, I heard him on his TV program say, 'Inhabitants of the swamp have over time become a federally protected species,' stressing the point that, 'Swamp creatures have become swamp fossils.'"

"Sounds like the FDA is one of the relics," Sam snickered.

"Seriously," Max asked, 'didn't the president recently appoint a new FDA commissioner to clean up their antics?"

"Yeah, that would be Dr. Scott Gottlieb. Refreshingly, he blamed the FDA as well for their delay in the distribution of generic drugs into the marketplace, citing their lack of a scientific and regulatory framework as well. At the same time, he admitted the FDA was not just a regulator, but a powerful tool used by Big PhRMA, helping it to maintain its monopolies. There's high hope among many that he'll be able to restore the FDA to a limited, less regulatory role. But they'll always be ineffective under the weight of Big PhRMA."

"The pharmaceutical industry is always chanting from the rooftops that they are highly regulated. Won't a limited, less regulatory role have the..."

"Yes, the fox will be watching the hen house."

"Sam, keeping with the animal metaphor, this case is turning you into a rabid dog. And I thought I was the cynic in this partnership."

"The more I read the worse it gets. Here's one last example. The FDA gave conditional approval for the drug Avastin to treat breast cancer. But a year later they rescinded the approval because the manufacturer, Genentech, could not prove it was effective. But between the time it was first released, and the FDA began the process to reverse their original decision, Genentech generated six billion dollars in sales—billion, with a "B"! The money was too good to let go. So Slater's counterpart, a man named Evan Morris, started an all-out campaign that delayed the process another year before it was finally taken off the shelves. Bit get this—during this time, it earned them another billion dollars. In total, it's reported that Genentech spent upwards of fifty million dollars a year on shaping government policy under the tutelage of Morris. But unlike Slater, Morris's embezzlement of millions of dollars was uncovered. The guy ended his life by blowing his brains out."

Max listened, although she had already concluded Big PhRMA was too big to fail. But to what extent they would go to protect their empire, was the trillion-dollar question. "It's a dangerous game they play. But as damning as the evidence appears, I still don't see them hiring assassins to kill doctors who are pushing natural products outside their purview." Max remained standing, alternating her sips of coffee with contemplation.

"What are you mulling over now?"

"Slater is the shill for Big PhRMA, and often times in a quasi-brotherly, quasi-bullying relationship with the FDA—but just maybe he's also the middleman for the Consortium."

"Christ! You really believe the Consortium is our missing link?"

An unsettling look blanketed her facial expression.

"What's wrong, Max?" Sam was becoming equally unsettled. Are you trying to tell me something? I'm finding you alarmingly difficult to read."

She sensed his angst, but her insides were churning. She could no longer hold back. "First!" she erupted, "they control our resources by perpetuating a climate change hoax! Now!—they utilize Big PhRMA in their Agenda 21 goal to control our population. How the hell could Noble accept such a utopian vision? And in a group whose strategy is to eliminate the *deplorables*—to kill their detractors at all costs?!"

"Where is this coming from? That bastard is gone. Noble is out of your life, even if the depraved organization lives on."

"Not Noble—Daniel."

"Princess, what are you talking about?"

"The man in the car was Daniel. I left to meet him…"

"You what?!"

Max held up her hand, thwarting off further anger. Then she calmed herself down and tried to reassure Sam that Daniel was there to make amends. She relayed the philosophical conversation that took place, trying to explain away her outburst. She omitted the implied threat for her to walk away from the investigation.

Sam was clearly pissed-off. First, for her not telling him sooner, and second, because he was absolutely sure she was withholding information from him. "Do you mind telling me what in the hell case we're trying to solve here?"

Max's phone rang, saved by the proverbial bell. "Hold on."

Sam gritted his teeth, waiting impatiently.

"Hey, Max, what have you found out about the senator's murder?" Ray asked.

"In all honesty, not much. Other than a beekeeper in Clovis, New Mexico, died from massive bee stings, but not enough actual bee stings to kill. But guess what, Chief—he had the same exact amount of bee venom in his bloodstream as the senator." Max winked in Sam's direction.

"Why do I not trust you, Max?"

"Thanks a lot!"

"Send me what you have so far. And make sure you keep me posted!"

"Will do." Max hit the *End Call* button.

"What was that all about?"

"Ray wanted to know if we found out anything more."

"True to form, I noticed you didn't tell all." Sam was still seething.

"There's nothing to tell until we're sure." Max smiled gently, "Please calm down. I'm sorry I didn't tell you. But back to answer your question; we're trying to find out who murdered Jeff. I'm convinced if we find the beekeeper's killer, we'll find Jeff's killer." *It can't be Daniel.* It was a vision she could not shake.

"We can't lose sight that many of these doctors and Big PhRMA have shared the same wrestling ring," Sam recalled as he attempted to control his anger.

"Agreed, but we can't make it our primary focus." She deliberately got off topic. "It's getting late. Tomorrow, see what you can find out about this guy named Sorenson. He could have been the last person to see Jeff alive. Also, try to contact the Japanese doctor; he should be back from his trip by now. I also want to know what he and the beekeeper were up to. I'll give Erin Elizabeth a call and see what relevant information she may have pertaining to our case. Then, I'm going to pay Slater a visit."

"That's all! Guess we have our work cut out for us as soon as we find the time to breathe."

Max could tell Sam was still displeased with her, but she braved it out and sat down instead of retreating.

"Is there something else you haven't told me?" Sam was almost afraid of the answer.

"What really happened to the assassin named L?" Max asked, as though she were asking about the weather.

"Whoa! Where's this coming from?"

"It's just been preying on my mind ever since I returned from Italy."

"You sure you really want to know?"

Max nodded.

Sam paused for a moment, and then made a full confession. "Jax called Erog and asked him to meet him at The Bachelor's Mill, knowing the weasel would send the assassin instead of doing the deed himself. Then, he asked me to meet him there..."

"Sam!"

"He thought it was time for two old buddies to work together again to protect your honor." Sam paused, noting Max's furrowed brow. "The hacked wiretaps from Erog's phone cited you as the next target. What choice did we have?"

Max remained expressionless.

"Honestly, I'm not sure what we would have done. But it didn't matter. When we got there, L was already dead. So, we took his phone, hoping it would trace back to Erog. Max, what brought all this up?" It was Sam's turn to be curious.

"I don't know. It's been a weird day. Forget it, let's get to work."

"You're the boss. But stay away from Daniel."

Max stood up and went back to her office.

Sam wasn't buying any of it.

Chapter 26

Girls' Night

The day was grueling. First, Max was forced to listen to Sam's long, drawn-out, morbid details of doctors dying. Her fortitude was in the full-test mode. Second, struggling to find a link between the doctors and Jeff's killer was taxing her patience. But given all they had uncovered, including the shenanigans of the monster pharmaceutical complex, she could not get the beekeeper out of her mind. The pressure was ratcheting up, but she was determined to stay focused. *The beekeeper must be the link,* she thought. She looked down at the open file folder, the one containing specific information she had gathered on Senator Lance. The photo printed on the obituary stared back. After a moment of reflection, she spoke out in frustration, "Argh, Jeff, what the hell did you get yourself into?!"

Buzzzzz!

The sound of the front door buzzer grabbed her attention. She automatically glanced at the security monitor. *Allison.* Max checked her watch to verify the time. Somehow it had already crept up to the eight o'clock hour. As was par for the course, Allison was on time. She quickly closed the file folder and went to the front door to greet her long-time friend.

"I see you're working late again. Do your office lights ever go off?"

"It's lovely to see you too!"

"Hey, Max, lighten up. Are you going to invite me in or do I have to stand out here on your doorstep?"

"Sorry, Sweetie, it's been a tough day. C'mon in. I'm ready to call it quits anyway."

Allison followed Max up the staircase to her apartment and into the kitchen.

"How about a glass of wine?"

"Perfect. Do you have any white? I'm kind of in that mood."

"Grab it out of the fridge and I'll get the glasses." As Max searched for two wine glasses without water stains left from her quick rinse method, she heard a shriek from across the room. "What's wrong?"

"Your refrigerator! It's disgusting. There's not one edible piece of food in here."

"What are you talking about?"

"Everything is processed with chemicals or preservatives. The cheeses, the meats, and all the drinks are loaded with sugar. Hawaiian Punch—seriously?"

"Grab me the bottle of Sokol Blosser's Pinot Gris—it's organic. And excuse me, when did you become such a health freak?"

"When Jeff almost…" Allison stopped mid-sentence. "Do you have a corkscrew?" she asked quickly to change the topic.

"I'll open it." Max took the bottle from her, uncorked the wine and poured two glasses. "Let's go in the living room. We both need to chill out."

Allison once again followed behind, refraining from conversation until they were seated.

"Cheers," Max offered, trying to lighten her mood.

"Cheers," Allison sighed.

"What's going on with you?"

"I just left my support group. It usually makes me a little edgy afterwards."

"Then why go? All you do is listen to everyone else's misery."

"Because it's helping. You know, it could help you too—to get over Noble."

"I don't need any help. I'm doing just fine, thank you."

"Sure you are. You work constantly. Other than that you have no life."

"Not true. I actually had dinner with Stanton last week." Max smiled, making it seem more than it was.

"Hmmm, how's that going?"

"Slow and casual. Enough of me. How are you really doing?"

"All in all—life sucks. I'm lonely, and I miss Jeff."

Max noted the change in Allison's expression. An unexpected calm washed across her face.

"What's up?"

Allison began to talk a bit more about her support group. But then she zoomed in on the discussions she thought might entice Max to want to join. Not taking the bait, she moved on and mentioned her new acquaintance.

"So he's why you go to these things?"

"I admit I look forward to the meetings, in part, to see him. But they're also helping."

"Oh, really," Max teased. Now she understood Allison's change in demeanor.

"It feels wonderful to have a man to talk with again. We have such fascinating conversations. And it doesn't hurt that he's attractive and quite charming."

"Wouldn't it be easier to just meet him at a café, or a hotel, and can all the morbid talk?"

"Knock it off. It's too soon."

"It's never too soon to move on with your life."

"Spoken from someone who hasn't moved on with her own life," Allison rebuffed.

"Well there's the pot calling the kettle black! Max hated where the conversation was heading. "Let's talk about the weather."

Allison gulped the rest of her wine and poured another glass. "How about you tell me what you found out about Jeff's killer?"

Max didn't care for the direction of this conversation either. She took a sip of wine to give herself a moment to think, and decided to give Allison a few tidbits. She was careful, however, to leave an honorable light shining on Jeff, and provide only enough information to give her comfort that the investigation was moving forward.

"I promise I'll let you know if there are any changes. Now, how about I order in some macrobiotic food?" Max smirked. "There's a great restaurant a few blocks away that delivers. It shouldn't take long."

Chapter 27

Demons in the Night

Slogging through the details of the doctor's deaths made the day gloomy. Girls' night with Allison was strained and awkward. The wee hours of the night were dreadful. Max's thoughts were discombobulated with visions of L sprawled out in the alley, Senator Spark lying on the park bench, a beekeeper with a swarm of bees hovering—and Jeff—and Noble. Daniel standing over the bodies took the limelight. Wrestling with these events left her numb; haunted by the sense of never being able to trust again. Even with Sam, she did not share every secret. Stanton, even less. It was all too byzantine.

"This is ridiculous. I need to stay focused," she admonished herself. The clock on her nightstand illuminated 3:00 a.m. She knew the case was slipping away. She grabbed her phone and texted: *call me,* and then laid back on her pillow and waited. Within seconds, her phone rang.

"Stanton?" she said with trepidation.

"Hi doll! It's great to hear from you, but it's my beddy time. Are you okay?"

"I'm lonesome."

"I'll be right over!"

"No! I just want to talk."

"Okay, would you like a little sexy talk?"

"Get serious, big boy. Have you ever heard of Solum?"

"Wow, that's quite a switch in conversation. Who are you messing with now?"

"It's just a name being tossed around. Curious, that's all."

"Max."

"Stanton."

"Okay, okay. Rumor on the street years ago was that he was a hired assassin credited with a zillion kills."

"I need a favor. Will you find out what POTUS knows about Solum?"

"Doll, I don't understand. If the president were to know anything about this guy, it's most certainly confidential. He won't share it with me."

"Rumor also has it he's CIA-trained."

"Then what about that new partner of yours? Wasn't he ex-CIA? He should be able find out what you want."

"It's a touchy subject with Sam. But I'm more interested in what the president knows. I think Solum bumped off Senator Spark and a fellow assassin named L. He may have killed Jeff as well."

"Max, you already seem to know an awful lot about this guy. Level with me; what have you really gotten yourself into?"

"Just find out, please?—and keep my name out of it."

"You're kidding, right?"

"Stanton."

"Why do I think you're not telling me everything?"

"Stanton."

"All right!—I'll see what I can find out. But please watch your back in the meantime."

"You're the best."

"Go back to sleep. Try to have some pleasant dreams this time."

The phone went dead. Max felt wholly inanimate. The one man she allowed herself to trust betrayed her. And although she cared for Stanton, and cared for Sam too, she would never let them enter her private world entirely. She even rationalized that holding back some pieces of the puzzle was a necessary precaution to keep them both safe.

Chapter 28

Beyond the Scope

Max was barely into her second energizing cup of coffee. And she was still plagued by her conversation with Stanton, fearful she had shared too much or too little. The annoying sound of the phone ringing only added more agitation to her self-inflicted mood.

"Max Ford."

"Good morning. My name is Erin Elizabeth. I'm returning your call."

"Ah, yes, yes, thank you for getting back to me."

"Your message said you were working on an investigation involving practitioners of alternative medicine," she said with heightened curiosity.

"I'm investigating the death of a friend who had been in contact with several of the doctors, on whose deaths you've reported."

"Which doctors?"

"I'm sorry; I can't give you the details while the investigation is ongoing. But it would be helpful to know who you believe is behind these mysterious deaths."

"Deaths or assassinations? It has been a long road trying to get the authorities to make the distinction. In fact, a well-respected doctor by the name of Coleen Huber sent a letter to the FBI asking them to investigate the series of assassinations of these alternative medical providers. To date, she's received no response. Since then, a total of eighty doctors have died, and many under suspicious circumstances. Now this epidemic to stifle alternative medicine has reached way beyond the medical community. In January of this year, Daniel Olmsted, a well known journalist and founder of *Age of Autism*, supposedly died of an overdose of prescription drugs. In November, less than a month ago, Jeana Beck, founder of *Unlocking Autism*, stepped out of her hotel room for a smoke and never returned to her child inside the hotel room. Her body was found in a canal behind the Rodeway Inn, in Lincoln City, Oregon, where they were staying. If you've been following my reports, then you know Dr. Bradstreet was a pioneer of reversing the effects of autism. And he was murdered days after being raided by the FDA. I'm sorry, but these events have deeply affected me. My partner is a holistic doctor and I'm afraid both of us are potential targets."

"It must be really scary." Max allowed, hearing the quiver in her voice.

"It breaks my heart each time I hear about another death. But I must keep reporting. Who will keep this message alive if I'm dead?"

The serious note in Erin's voice was telling. She not only invested her heart, but her soul into this quest that could jeopardize her life. But one word she said stood out.

"Erin, you said assassinations. Who do you believe is orchestrating them? And why?" Max had her own theory, but needed confirmation—something to signal she and Sam were not so far off the mark.

"I won't speculate. I'm only reporting. I just don't want other doctors to live in fear. Many practitioners closed their offices or hired bodyguards based on these reports. I understand it's necessary to be aware and safe, but I hope those brave enough to work in the field of holistic medicine will carry the torch and continue to do great work in memory of those we've lost over the last two years." Erin went silent for a moment, and then asked, "Who do you believe is killing these doctors?"

Max was tongue-tied, not expecting the question to boomerang. "In all honesty—I don't know right now—I'm only bouncing around theories. However, if I'm able to prove anything that may be helpful to you, I promise to be back in contact. I appreciate your time and for the valiant work you're doing."

"Thank you, Miss Ford."

"Please call me Max. And let's stay in touch" She ended the call.

Sam blasted into Max's office, scaring the living daylights out of her.

"Sam!"

"Hey, have you seen the morning paper?"

"No!"

"What's the matter, princess?"

"Aside from your grand entrance—bad night. And I just got off the phone with Erin Elizabeth."

"Really! Did you get anything useful out of her?"

"She said she's only reporting the deaths, and will not speculate as to who may be orchestrating the killings."

"Believe her?"

"Not sure. But she's clearly spooked. So, what did I miss that prompted you to barge into my office?"

"There was a reported plane crash in the Amazon jungle. The pilot was killed; no passengers. But our headline is that the pilot's name was Brad Johansson."

"Amazon!"

"Ring a bell?"

"Not past the fog at this hour. Fill me in."

"Remember back about ten years ago, a group of scientists at the FDA's Center for Devices and Radiological Health alleged safety problems with the colonoscopy and breast cancer devices. It had to do with the level of radiation exposure. As far as it was reported, the FDA ignored their warnings and approved the medical devices."

"Vaguely. Wasn't it developed by General Electric's Healthcare Division?"

"Yes, and the same company that made over three billion dollars a year from its diagnostic products. But the huge scandal that developed quashed the initial complaint. The real hubbub was the discovery that the FDA was monitoring the scientist's computers and leaking confidential information. In the end, the case was dismissed, and the scientists' reputations were smeared. And GE's profits were protected."

"I remember the name of one of the whistleblowers was Brad Johansson."

"You win the prize!"

"For what?" Max was still puzzled.

Sam turned the newspaper around and flashed a photo of the dead pilot.

"You're kidding. That guy fits Sorenson's description."

"Thought the same thing. So I faxed a copy of the photo to the clerk at the Seringal Hotel to be sure. He got right back and confirmed it was the same man who met Jeff in the lobby. I also sent the photo to the Curry County Sheriff. He showed it to Miss Ellie who confirmed the man in the photo was the same *fella that kept poppin' up unannounced* at the apiary."

"So, Brad Johansson and Sorenson are one and the same?"

"From what I could dig up, Johansson was extremely dissatisfied with the outcome in the General Electric case and took on the FDA as his pet project. He was a busy boy becoming a whistleblower's best friend. In one case, he worked with a sales rep named Kurt Kroening who sued Forest Laboratories and its subsidiary, Forest Pharmaceuticals, claiming they paid kickbacks to physicians, rewarding them based on the number of prescriptions they'd write for the firm's drugs. The *Kurt Kroening v. Forest Laboratories* case settled for thirty-eight-million dollars. In another instance, in *Peggy Ryan v. Endo Pharmaceuticals, Inc.*, Ryan received valuable information from our inside man that helped her prove the company was illegally marketing a pain-treatment patch called Lidoderm. That suit ended in a whopping one-hundred-ninety-three-million-dollar settlement."

"I'm surprised Johansson survived this long."

"His days were numbered. He eventually ran out the clock when he blew the lid off the FDA expediting the approval of orphan drugs."

"Our man caused quite a stir."

"So much so, Johannsson ended up on the FDA's secret watchlist, which explains his low profile. What's peculiar, is since these multiple incidents of whistleblowing, the FDA launched a public website for whistleblowers, supposedly to make it easier to report misconduct."

"Or perhaps provide them with advance warning," Max concluded.

"Isn't that an oxymoron?"

"Thank you, professor. But if Johansson was showing up in both Brazil and New Mexico, he must have used fake credentials under the name of Sorenson. They probably figured it out and were hot on his trail. Obviously, it led them to the beekeeper and then on to Brazil and then on to Jeff. Now—all three are dead."

"Max, I know we're still theorizing, but when you said *they*, I don't think you were using it in the generic sense. Who are they?"

"You know I've been hesitant to pin these murders or even consider the alleged murders of holistic doctors on Big PhRMA."

"Yes, but Slater led us in that direction. I'm sure it wasn't his intent, but with the Feds closing the Clovis Hill Apiary, and given what's happened to Bradstreet, it makes for a powerful case."

"Even though my virtual dots are still flying all over the place, I can't stop from connecting them back to a group—one even more powerful than the government."

"You mean the *Deep State*? The Consortium?" Every time Sam mentioned the name of the nefarious group, the hairs stood upright on the back of his neck. Not because of the untold havoc the group reportedly reaped, but the fact that he and Max may be tangling with them again.

Max mentally deliberated before answering. "Absent my crystal ball, I'm ready to conclude that the Consortium is in the driver's seat or at the helm of the pharmaceutical industry—and they're using Slater as a middleman to carry out their global strategy."

"Well, princess, you let the cat out of the climate-change bag on your last case. Are you really prepared to challenge population control as well?"

"What we know, without a doubt, is Big PhRMA has both unprecedented economic and political power. Their trillion-dollar war chest also made it possible to create a societal addiction to drugs that only mask symptoms—but does nothing to cure the diseases. On reflection, that would accomplish the Consortium's goal of population control—in fact, do the trick." Hearing her own words left her dismayed by the inhumanity of it all.

"Speaking of cures, I had an engaging chat with Dr. Mizukami."

"You did? When?" Max was seeking a positive note in the conversation.

"About four o'clock this morning. I came down with the Max syndrome and I couldn't sleep. Anyway, he said he's treated over four thousand advanced cancer patients in the last thirty-five years using an ethanol-extracted propolis from a Brazilian plant called Baccharis Dracunculifolia."

"Bravo, you said the jawbreaker!"

"I had to roll it over my tongue a few times first." Sam admitted. "The doctor explained that this particular plant contains a higher concentration of propolis including antioxidants—specifically, artepillin C, an ingredient that inhibits cancer-cell growth. He was adamant that he combines both conventional and alternative medicine. Like the senator, he believes in removing the cancer surgically, but he's not completely against chemo and radiation therapy. However, he also believes his use of propolis, which possesses direct anti-cancer agents, increases the survival rate. In fact, he said it produces an antiangiogenic effect in the same way chemical anti-cancer agents function."

"Huh!"

"In layman's terms, it shuts off the blood supply to the tumor and inhibits it from growing. He also reported that it's antiviral and antibacterial, which helps to regenerate healthy tissues faster. His list was endless about the positive effects of propolis. And with over five hundred of his patients on this protocol, he claimed amazing results. Hold on a second. Let me grab my notes."

Sam shuffled through the hen scratches he called handwriting and pulled up the notes he made during the call.

"The doctor said the survival rate of his patients who took propolis tended to be disease-free, sometimes double, triple, or even ten times longer than expected. A few patients with cancer tumors, one centimeter or less in diameter, had them completely disappear without conventional treatment. He also mentioned that patients using propolis in combination with chemotherapy or radiation tend to exhibit better treatment results and less adverse reactions compared to only conventional therapy. Do you have time to listen to a few case studies?"

"I'm all ears."

"In 1998, he had a forty-six-year-old female with hepatitis C who subsequently developed hepato cell carcinoma. Her liver CT scan revealed three tumors of one centimeter in diameter. He recommended ten thousand milligrams of propolis be taken daily. Her liver tumors totally disappeared two months later."

"Wow."

"A year earlier, he had a fifty-two-year-old female diagnosed with scirrhous-type stomach cancer. It was stage III, and the doctors had given her a one-year survival rate of only ten percent. She had a stomach resection to remove the cancer that had metastasized. After the procedure, she also took a daily dose of ten thousand milligrams of propolis. She has had no recurrence these past years since the procedure."

"Now, one more story. In 2003, a forty-six-year-old male fractured his pelvic bone and was diagnosed with multiple myeloma at stage IV. His estimated five-year survival rate was twenty-five percent. That patient took forty-five thousand milligrams of propolis every day during treatment. He then underwent four cycles of chemotherapy, but exhibited no adverse reactions. His white blood count remained normal. He's been in complete remission. I could go on, but you get the point."

"Impressive. So propolis even lessened the side effects of chemotherapy. Did you get anything else out of the dear doctor?"

"Funny you should ask. The overall conversation was actually quite pleasant, and as you heard, informative—at least until I mentioned his visit to the Clovis Hill Apiary."

"And…?"

"He clammed up. I tried prodding, but I think I pushed too hard. His last words before he hung up were to tell Max Ford to back away."

"What is it with these guys? The more they tell me to back off, the more I fire the jets full steam ahead! Little do they know, I hit the afterburners, not the brakes!"

Max appeared to be overly touchy, but Sam left her reaction unchallenged. He still wanted to pry that other morsel of information he knew she was holding back. But he decided patience was paramount when trying to out spy another spy.

Max looked at her watch. "Got to go; I'll be late for my appointment."

"You really think it's smart? Slater is about as close to the lion's den as you'd want to get. If you're right about him, he's certainly on to us—or maybe he craves your charming company."

"Perish the thought, but I need to be sure." Max shrugged her shoulders. "Maybe, I've got this guy all wrong. I'll be back in a while."

"Give yourself time for a shower afterwards."

Chapter 29

Standing Ground

Max headed back to her office to collect her bag and her thoughts, in that order, until she was interrupted by the sound of her phone ringing.

Max saw the name of the caller and immediately loosened her emotional armor. "Stanton, what a pleasant surprise."

"Hey, doll, where are you?"

"I'm in my office, but I'm heading out for an appointment. Why?"

"Cancel it. POTUS wants to see you alone ASAP. Meet me out front in five."

"Stanton. Stanton. Damn." She had only four minutes to sulk before grabbing her bag and leaving to meet her self-appointed chauffeur. "See ya, Sam," she shouted as she dashed out the front door.

Stanton stood beside the passenger door, holding it open waiting for her. "You're lookin' beautiful as usual."

"Thanks," she said with a hint of a smile, and then crawled into the back seat.

Stanton sat in the driver's seat and quickly asked, "Why would POTUS want to see you?"

"Except to help him solve world problems, I don't know why the president wants to spend time with me."

"I can think of a reason."

"Be careful—you guys are getting into a whole lot of *exposé heartache* these days."

"Does that mean I can't call you doll anymore?"

"Handsome, you can call me anything you want." She caught him smiling at her in the rearview mirror and flashed a wink back. She knew he was only messing with her, but fun time was over.

"Stanton, be serious. POTUS and I don't chit-chat on a regular basis, so I have no clue what he wants. But when you asked him about Solum the other night, you left my name out of it, right?"

"I'd protect the president with my life. But you, doll, will always come first. And no, your name did not enter the conversation."

Max remained quiet as she stared into his eyes reflecting from the mirror. Her thoughts questioned whether she had rattled the lion's cage with her inquiry.

Stanton broke the silence. "You were right, though. Solum was CIA. In fact, he became the gold standard for their trained assassins. From the grapevine, he went rogue years ago and ended up on the CIA hitlist. Then there were reports that a CIA operative was credited with his kill. And the case was closed. About two years ago, however, rumors began to swirl that Solum was still alive. But the upper echelon think the recent assassinations attributed to him are only copycats."

"So, they're not looking for him anymore."

Stanton heard a strange calm in her voice, something he found incongruous. But there was no time to inquire as he turned off Pennsylvania Avenue and headed up the drive to 1600. There was no delay as they sailed through the front gate. And Max received her visitor's pass, with no questions asked. Being escorted by the head of the president's secret service detail was a definite plus. Within seconds, Stanton pulled up to the main entrance of the White House and got out of the car to open her door. "Don't sweat it! I'll wait for you here."

Max turned and headed into *the official* oval-shaped lion's den.

"Hello, Max," the president greeted as he stood up from behind his desk. "It's nice to see you again."

"Mr. President, it's always my pleasure to spend time with you."

"Please be seated, Max. I understand you're involved in an investigation that could have you in a continuing combat with the director of the Consortium. I have to ask you to back away."

"With all due respect, sir, this concerns the death of a US Senator."

"It's a petty squabble between Big PhRMA and a beekeeper. The senator should not have been involved. It was beyond his realm."

Max was stunned at first by how much the president was aware of; both of the issue and the players. Then again, he was the president.

"But, sir…"

"I'm trying to keep the Consortium under control. I'm working deals, but Max, you keep getting in the way. I don't need any impediments. It's complicated enough."

"Mr. President, considering they have threatened my life twice, do you mind explaining their precise roles? What does the Consortium have to do with Jeff's death exactly?" She had her own suspicions, but wanted to hear from the man himself.

"Just because Maurice Strong died doesn't mean Agenda 21 is also dead. The UN's goal is still to promote its tenets, but there's another, even more powerful surviving group pulling the strings. They're worse than terrorists. They have the power to restructure the world. You've witnessed their wizardry of misdeeds. In comparison, Strong's original strategy is akin to a pea shooter."

"Are you speaking of global governance, Mr. President?" She knew he was, but nevertheless she prodded.

"All you need to know is that the director is the conductor, and the Consortium is the orchestra. Granted your last case helped to expose their climate-change hoax. And need I remind you at what cost?" The president moved beyond the rhetorical question and cautioned, "Now you're treading in the dangerous waters of population control."

"Where do they get their unlimited power?"

"Their power comes from their unlimited resources."

"How is that possible?"

"Many ways—black budget, binary options market, crypto-currency tracking."

"Sir…"

"Max, I enjoyed our philosophical conversation, but there's nothing more you need to know—other than they're untouchable. And certainly, beyond the reach of an individual sleuth wandering around a mine field. No reflection on your character or your competence."

"Mr. President…"

"Max! I am only one world leader. I'm utilizing every capability I have to keep them at bay—but you're not helping."

"Slater came to you?" She looked for a reaction. *Come on, confirm he's the middleman.*

The president offered a stern warning rather than an answer. "You're trying my patience, Max. Trust me, I'll handle this—my way—and for the US population I swore to protect."

Max stood her ground, but resorted to a less confrontational approach. "Sir, we are talking about the murder of Senator Jeffrey Lance. You delivered his eulogy. You were his friend."

"That's true, but irrelevant. I'm ordering you to walk away from your investigation, however problematic it may be for you."

Oddly enough, the president's calm response put Max even more ill at ease. She began to wonder whether he was actually aware that Daniel was her brother. Treading cautiously, she asked if he had any idea who assassinated Jeff.

"We believe a man that goes by the codename Solum was hired by the Consortium. You do not want to tangle with this guy. Trust me."

He doesn't know, she thought, trying not to show her great relief.

"Max, thank you for coming." The president held her hand between his and looked directly into her eye. "Please, I don't want you to become another casualty."

Max took her cue. Any further questioning would be unproductive. "Good day, Mr. President."

When she left the White House, Stanton was standing by, waiting as promised. He noticed her discomfort. Whether out of fear or anger, he could not tell.

"C'mon, doll. Let's get you out of here."

Max mumbled, "So that's why he threatened me. He's trying to save me." The haunting vision of Daniel returned.

"Who threatened you? You forgot to mention that minor detail."

"Home, Stanton."

He followed orders and gave her time to recover from whatever conversation she had with POTUS. It had a visible affect. She was mute the entire ride back to her Victorian, but he monitored her from the mirror. She did not seem to notice.

"Here you are, home, safe and sound."

"Thanks, Stanton." Max grabbed the door handle.

"Max, wait a minute. I don't know what's going on, but let's go in and talk about it." Stanton started to exit the car.

"No! Let's stay here in the car."

He turned around and reached for her hand. She resisted.

"Solum was the hired assassin who killed Noble. He also killed Spark and Jeff. He also was…" Max paused.

Stanton gave her the time needed, as she was apparently taking him into her confidence.

"He was the one who tried to kill you. Thank God he missed your heart."

It was Stanton's time to back away into silence.

Max just stared at him.

"So, you're tracking him?" Stanton asked in disbelief. "No offense, but I think this is above your pay grade."

"I've been told to walk away from the case, but I have to bring him in for reasons I can never explain."

"I suggest you listen to whomever is giving you advice, especially if it's coming from POTUS. He has the bigger picture. It truly is time to back off."

"Why does everyone tell me to back off?! You've learned firsthand what that means."

"Yes, you'll dig your stilettos in deeper. Seriously, Max, what are you thinking?!"

"The case has metastasized into much more. Slater keeps popping up in the background, which drags Big PhRMA into the picture. I'm trying to figure out Solum's role. All fingers point to him. But a man with a scar on his left cheek killed the beekeeper. Solum doesn't have one."

"How do you know? And I thought this was about finding Jeff's killer?"

Max reached for the handle again. This time opening the door. Stanton began to follow suit and get out of the car.

"Stop, I'll call you later."

"Promise me you'll consider the warnings and set your obstinate pride aside. I want you in one piece. You know doll, I never stopped loving you." He pledged to himself he would not push to restore their broken relationship, but she needed to be certain he would be there for her.

"Thanks for the ride, Stanton."

He let her get out of the car, but he stared intently as she ascended the steps to her home.

Chapter 30

The Ultimatum

Slater's other cellphone rang. He knew the caller. He knew the question.

"Yes, Director, he's dead. It was a plane crash that will be deemed pilot error."

"How can you be sure he was the one?"

"He had to have been the leaker. We had him on surveillance, in and out of the apiary, and at the hotel in Manaus. Sir..." Slater hesitated.

"What is it?"

"Max Ford scheduled a meeting with me today."

"She what?!"

"Sir, she's only on a fishing expedition. I figured what's the harm to placate her." Slater knew this was not going to end well, but he sucked it up and blurted it out. "Then she cancelled. A few minutes later, the head of POTUS's secret service picked her up and took her to the White House."

"Enough of this madness! Take care of her and her sidekick once and for all!"

The sound of the phone receiver hitting its cradle reverberated in his ear. Slater knew it was never healthy to alienate the director, though he seemed to be a large contributor to the director's aggravation in recent days. Once again, Slater was forced to pick up the cudgel and placed another undesirable call.

"Solum, it's time. She's getting too deep into our business. And now she's put us back on POTUS's radar. It's time to take care of her, along with her spook partner, Casper.

"Slater, I'm tired of cleaning up your messes. I'm out!"

"Solum—you don't seem to understand—there is no exit door you'll ever be able to walk through. Now take care of them!"

"I'll threaten her. I'll get her to back away. But I'm not killing her."

"You have a thing for this PI? She's nothing but trouble. She's like a magnet always attaching herself to our business."

"If Max Ford disappears, all hell will break loose. She's developed extremely powerful friendships in high places. And before they go after the director—they're going to come after you. Who knows, they might even hire me to do it." Solum enjoyed the moment.

"This is a firm order from the director."

"Well, the director is not thinking straight. But you are—aren't you Slater? Look, I'll convince her to walk away. It will be over for now."

"Just do it!"

Chapter 31

Shattered Fate

The room appeared to be spinning out of control as she attempted to put all the pieces of the puzzle together. She figured out the who, the what, the why, the where and even the how—but there was no solid evidence to prove it—there was nothing watertight. That sinking wave of doubt was moving in fast and she could not stop it. *Is it really over?* she questioned. But she dismissed the thought immediately and opted for another recount.

It was obvious that many of the doctors' deaths were suspect. That for Big PhRMA the stakes were high. That the FDA worked closely with this pharmaceutical behemoth. That the beekeeper and Jeff were killed by the same assassin. Max hesitated with her outpouring of thoughts, but she could not evade the most troubling conclusion. *And Solum was involved and by way of extension, the Consortium. Both an intrinsic part of the strategy.*

All the facts without the hard evidence left her in a state of despair. She arched back in her chair and then at once bolted forward, startled by the doorbell. "Can I help you," she asked curtly, annoyed at the intrusive face staring at her from the other side of the security monitor.

"FedEx delivery ma'am," he responded, waving an envelope in the air.

"One minute." Unnerved for more reasons than she understood, she looked inside her desk drawer and eyed her Sig Sauer. *Snap out it, Max. It's just a delivery guy.* When she opened the door the guy was gone, but the envelope was lying on the doormat. "Aren't we impatient," she uttered as she walked back to her desk with the package. "Now what!"

Inside the envelope was a plane ticket.

"Odd."

Even odder was the note enclosed. It read: **Help us finish what Senator Lance started**. The note was unsigned, but she recognized the logo, the one for the American Beekeeping Federation. Renewed hoped suddenly replaced her despair, shining a new light on the possibility of a positive outcome. She stared at the ticket and the arrival city.

Buzzzzz!

"What is it now!" She looked at the monitor again. This time a sharp pang hit her chest as she viewed the visitor. On impulse, she looked inside her desk drawer for a second time. But this time she pulled out the Sig Sauer and tucked it inside the back of her waistband. She felt a chill go up her spine, but it was not the cold metal pressed against her skin that caused the sensation. Max steadied her hand and hit the buzzer, releasing the lock at the front door.

Daniel stepped inside.

Max was thunderstruck as she stared at the mutilation on his left cheek.

Daniel noticed and ran his hand along the discolored ridge. "A great disguise, don't you think?" Little by little he peeled off the prosthetic scar.

She did not respond. *He killed Jeff* was her foremost numbing thought. Then she moved her attention from his cheek to study his eyes. "Why are you here? To settle an old score? Or run an errand for the Consortium?"

"Dear sister, you made a horrible mistake thinking Erog was the messenger. Instead, your interference forced the director to the brink and to take his own life."

Max shot him a questioning look, but said nothing. She wondered why he would bring up the subject.

"The director was never to be revealed. You'll find the next director to be more formidable."

"Daniel, what do want from me?"

"You simply have to stop snooping around. I warned you before to get lost! Trust me; there's no way you can win this one."

She had contemplated those same words, but hearing them again only made her more determined. As Stanton said, *dig her stilettos in deeper.* "What are you talking about?"

"You can't bring down Big PhRMA."

"Who says I'm trying to bring down PhRMA? I'm investigating the senator's death."

"Back down! Or I can't promise you'll get out of this one alive."

"Daniel, piss off!"

"I'm trying to save your life, dammit!"

"I still can't believe you're their hired killer. You're the one who needs to walk away. Make this right."

"You don't walk away from the director or the director's loyal followers."

Once again, the horrible visions of their father lying dead on the sofa, the senator lying on the park bench in the same fashion, both with a gun at their fingertips, spun in her head like a carousel out of control. The sickening reality hit her. "That's why you had me meet you in the park. At the same place where you killed Senator Spark." The thought fate had brought them together in such a horrible twisted fashion left her detached for the moment.

"It was my job to take out Spark. L was to take care of the rest." Daniel paused. "But he blew it when he failed to kill you—and that scientist you were protecting—so I was ordered to take him out." An out-of-place smile crossed his face. "You have to admire the irony."

"Why are you telling me this?"

"Because you are the only one who knows the whole truth; but you're living on borrowed time."

"No, I mean, why are you admitting what you've done?"

"Why not? If you turn me in, it all comes out. When the CIA finds out you are Claudia Irving, then you'll become a greater threat. And the perfect bargaining chip to be used by the Consortium. I can only imagine the director's face if the truth were to be known."

"I don't understand."

"They'd have to assume I've confessed all my sins, implicating them along the way. Both the CIA and the Consortium. There will be absolutely nothing I can do to protect you at that point—enough of this brotherly-sisterly chit-chat. Max, this is your last warning."

"Or what? You'll, what is it you say, 'take me out'?"

"First, I'll start with your friend. I've enjoyed getting to know her, but she's expendable."

"Allison! So you're the one she met at the support group! For God's sake, leave her out of this!"

The change in Daniel's expression caused her body to shudder. The sinister smile made her insides churn with revulsion. It was hard for her to fathom that her own flesh and blood was a cold-hearted killer—and that he could be so cruel.

"Let this be your last warning. Gotta go, sis." The look on Daniel's face changed. It was counter to his earlier menacing expression. He stared a moment longer and then turned and headed for the front door.

"Solum! Stop!"

He cocked his head back in her direction.

Max stood in a prone position; her gun aimed directly at him.

His peculiar expression returned. "This dance again!"

"I'll give you what you want! But leave Allison alone! And let this be your warning."

Suddenly, an explosion of etched glass shattered through the air. Max stood frozen as she felt parts of her own life shatter into a thousand pieces.

Daniel grabbed his arm and spun around. He was gone.

When Sam arrived, it was patently obvious that the front door had been blown to smithereens, sending him straight into a frenzy. "Max," he shouted, as he rushed in with his own weapon drawn.

Max was seated on the sofa, with her gun clasped to her chest. She could see Sam rush toward her over the broken glass, but her body did not react. She had no idea whether she had been sitting there for a few minutes or hours. And Sam sounded like he was in an echo chamber.

"Max, what happened?" The fright in his voice was apparent, but he tried to remain calm. He surveyed the scene one more time. Any attempt to solicit information from her was unsuccessful. "Max, snap out of it!" he yelled. His shouting had no effect and finding no other recourse, he resorted to shaking her shoulders looking for a reaction.

"Sam, stop shaking me!"

"Do you mind telling me what the bejesus happened here? There's a bloody trail halfway down the street."

"Blood! Oh my God—I really did shoot him."

"I doubt it's life-threatening. From the amount of blood, you most likely just grazed him. But who the hell is *him*?"

Max rocked back and forth, trying to regain her senses. She had to focus on her next assignment. She gave it careful thought before responding. "The Consortium sent Daniel to scare me off the investigation."

"And?!"

"I told him I'd back off!"

"And then you shot him. Nice touch. But what are you really going to do?"

"Back off!"

"Max, you're definitely not sounding like yourself, nor are you making much sense."

"Perhaps it's time we move on."

"I'd like to believe you, but you don't give up that easily."

"You know as well as I do, there's no way to prove who is actually responsible for the deaths of the beekeeper and Jeff. All we know is that the beekeeper was illegally growing a plant to make propolis. That purpose—died with him. Look, I've tangled with the Consortium before, just as you have. And, do I need to remind you that when we were running around Italy trying to protect a scientist, we were almost killed in the process. I'm on their hit list, most likely you are too. It's not worth it. Let's get back to investigating cases we can solve."

"I can't believe you're really backing down; we're so close."

"You can't win them all."

"If you're not going to pursue this case further, why don't you at least bring POTUS up-to-date."

"You're kidding! With his twitter fingers on steroids, he's likely to put more people in harm's way." The last thing Sam needed to find out was that she had already been hauled into the Oval Office and warned to stay away. "Look, I'm convinced doctors are being killed because they discovered ways to save lives without putting money into the pockets of the pharmaceutical companies. It's insane, I know, but we have no proof. Besides, Erin Elizabeth is determined to prove there's a conspiracy. So, we'll let her do the legwork. If we need to jump back in, we'll reevaluate the ramifications at that time.

In the meantime, I'm turning over what evidence we have on Jeff's death to the Capitol Police. Let them run with it. As far as this case goes—I'm done!"

"Max, we're so close on this one." Sam goaded. At the same time, he was taken aback by his own admission. He wanted to see the case through to the end.

"It's not up for discussion—it's over."

Sam relented, knowing she was right. They needed to walk away while they still had legs that could carry them. "You're the boss. I'll go get the broom and clean up this mess."

"Thanks. And while you're still pissed off at me, you might as well know I'm going out of town for a few days. I'll need you to hold down the fort."

"With Stanton?"

"No."

"Max, it may not be safe out there. How can you be sure this is over, just because you stepped down? They can still come after you. Your back can still carry a bullseye."

"They won't!" Max headed for her office, ending the conversation.

Sam left it unchallenged; he could only fight so many battles in any given day. But it did not negate his lingering concerns.

Max felt horrible for not telling him the truth—the part that she was not retreating from the case. Aside from that, she believed for some inexplicable reason, Daniel would keep her safe.

Chapter 32

The Beekeeper's Secret

The plane landed at the International Airport in Monterrey, Mexico, on schedule. Within minutes of pulling up to the gangway, Max headed to another gate to wait for a flight scheduled to leave for Sao Paolo, Brazil. She assumed her final destination was Manaus, but thus far it appeared to be a round-about and lengthy flight pattern. The detailed instructions she received earlier from Dr. Harold Johnson, however, were clear. It was also clear she had no logical choice but to accept her new assignment. She checked her watch; one more hour before takeoff.

"Excuse me, Miss Ford," said the woman standing before her.

Max looked up and gaped with a surprised expression. It was not the presence of this intrusive woman or the fact she knew her name that was unsettling—it was her appearance. Max thought she was looking at a mirror image of herself. In a flash, Dr. Johnson's instruction became clear, right down to her attire. Both were wearing a pair of jeans and a white sweater with a black leather jacket opened to reveal a red scarf loosely coiled around their necks.

"These are for you." The woman wheeled two large metal totes in front of Max and then swooped into the seat next to her. On both sides of each tote, emblazoned with large stickers printed with the words: **Property of the U.S. Government**. Max's uneasiness elevated. The look-a-like then handed her a piece of paper with an address. "You will have only six hours to make the delivery. The drive will take you nearly four and a half hours to reach your destination. Do you understand?"

"Not exactly." Max was still bewildered.

Without responding, the woman handed her a passport and a driver's license. On both documents, the name Simone Tattler was inscribed next to a not so attractive photo of Max. Even more disturbing; it was a diplomatic passport.

"Not bad!" Max said, curious as to what was next.

"There's a Hertz rental-car waiting for you. It's best you leave now. You will find further instructions in the glove compartment."

In a sudden moment of revelation, it hit her. She was not headed to Manaus. She was going to drive across the Mexican border with fake I.D. and God knows with what contraband, to who the hell knows where.

"I'll need your ticket," the woman stated with a stretched-out hand.

"So, you're traveling back to Sao Paolo as Maxine Ford."

The statement was not a question, and the imposter understood. She scooted off to stand in line to wait for the announcement for first class passengers to board.

Max scurried out of the terminal and off to the Hertz ticket counter.

When she approached the border crossing at Nueva Ciudad Guerrero, she let out a few deep yoga breaths to calm her nerves while she envisioned the totes stored in the trunk. Easing up on the brake she moved another car length ahead and edged closer to the immigration kiosk. She was third in line. Again, she inhaled and then let the air out of her lungs in a slow measured pattern.

"Passport, senorita," asked the border agent with the smarmy smile.

Max returned a courteous expression, but nothing too inviting, and waited for the agent to flip through the passport. She had noticed earlier that the passport was reminiscent of a well-traveled document, filled with stamps from around the world. *Thorough,* she thought, once again admiring the handiwork.

As the agent ran through the usual list of 'are you transporting' items, Max responded no to each question, despite the fact she had no clue.

"Open your trunk, por favor," he ordered, expecting her to hit a button.

Max had to make sure he would not try to open the cases and feigned stupidity as a reason to get out of the car. "It's a rental car. I think I have to use the key." The agent didn't argue, and from the way he eyed her, she assumed he took it as an opportunity to give her a once-over. She took full advantage that time and offered a genuine, slightly, more alluring smile.

She opened the trunk in a relaxed manner, trying to be as nonchalant as possible.

"And what's in there?" he asked, seeming less friendly than before.

"Sorry. I'm not the official courier," she responded and then proceeded to deliver her rehearsed lines. "I've been instructed by the U.S. Consulate General in Santa Catarina to deliver them to the U.S. State Department in Houston. I was not given the combination to the locks."

Agitated, he looked at her passport again and eyed her more closely. Then he refocused on the government seals. Using his better judgement, he chose not to pursue it further, most likely to avoid an international skirmish. For certain, the two countries did not need another incident. He closed the trunk and handed Max back her passport. "Buenos dias." He tipped his hat and walked back to the kiosk, waved her on, and approached the next car.

Max, not giving her luck a second thought, drove across the border to Falcon Heights, Texas. Safe, back inside her own country, she headed off finally to learn the purpose behind her clandestine mission. She made good time getting to Corpus Christi in just a little over two hours. Now as she eased through the streets in the Flour Bluff district, she could not help but notice the remnants of damage that Hurricane Harvey had left in its wake. It was painful to see such devastation, even after several months had passed. She continued to make her way to the docks near the Industrial Canal through the deserted and run-down area. The GPS indicated five more minutes with no sign of the terrain improving. Max was having misgivings, but she was at the point of no return. Then, out of nowhere, her apprehension turned to exhilaration. She sensed that she was about to find out the vital missing piece of the unsolved puzzle.

Max drove up to the massive corrugated steel warehouse on the left, marked with the number 3666. The door to the building was left ajar. When she entered the first floor, it was totally desolate, absent of any lighting. Only subtle hues from the setting sun shed light through the large windows, casting a shadow on a man standing across the giant room.

"You're a welcome sight!" he called out.

"Dr. Harold Johnson, I presume," she responded, to the unidentifiable person.

"At your service."

Max headed in his direction, noting the pigeons cooing above. She hoped they were the only creatures swirling over her head. At the same time, she tried to dodge the massive pools of unknown liquid spotting the floor. Wheeling the two heavy totes, traversing them through an obstacle course only added to her woes. But as she shortened the distance between herself and the doctor, she could tell he was a well-seasoned gentleman, estimating his age to be in the seventies.

"Let me help you with those. We still have quite a hike."

"Before I hand over the totes, I want to know what's in them." The pleasantries were quaint, but she'd gone through a hell of a lot and was impatient to know why.

"You've earned the right. But first, please follow me so we can join the others." He moved in to help her with the cargo.

"I'm fine, thank you."

"Suit yourself."

Hal turned and continued across the massive room to another steel door. Passing through the entryway they approached a metal staircase, at which point Max reluctantly surrendered one of the totes. But she took great care with the other as she warily stepped down into a black hole.

"Where are we going?" she asked. Her queasy feeling did not abate, even though they were back on solid ground.

"Follow me. We're almost there."

Her trepidation increased as she trudged through a long, dark, secret, underground tunnel, with the doctor using his phone to light the way. The saving grace was that Max could only see in front of where she was walking because there was a putrid smell— its origin she preferred not to know.

"Here we are," Hal announced.

At last they reached another staircase, similar to the one they had walked down. This one however, presented a greater challenge as they edged themselves up the steps with the two totes, for what must have been three stories high.

Max remained silent as she maneuvered the one tote with the unknown cargo until at last they reached another door. The doctor led the way into a room that seemed out of place, considering the abandoned condition of the building she had first entered. What surprised her most was the humongous long wooden table with the large group of men seated on both sides. It reminded her of a corporate boardroom, but the men bore no resemblance to typical captains of industry.

"Gentlemen, the package has arrived."

Hal proceeded to introduce her to each of the men as they stood up around the long conference table. There was a surprising mix of doctors, along with representatives of the American Honey Producers Association and the American Beekeeping Federation. They were all dressed in white lab coats. Placed in front of each of them were large acrylic boxes.

"Miss Ford..."

"Please call me Max," she interjected robotically.

"Certainly, Max. Now to answer your questions.

Hal opened the two cases. Inside were boxes with plexiglass covers perforated with tiny holes. There was a strange sound coming from within the containers.

"This case contains young drones that will become sexually mature within the next few days, which is why the timing was so vital. This other case holds the finest virgin queens waiting to be bred. These are extraordinarily unique bees that come from hives deep in the Amazon jungle. Their breeding dates back thousands of years."

"Bees. You had me play this cloak and dagger game for a bunch of bees?"

"Max, you've gone to great lengths to investigate the murders of Oliver Prince, Senator Lance, and you know what happened to Sorenson. It was with Sorenson's help..."

"Excuse me, Sorenson was FDA."

Hal chuckled. "Max, he was working with us. He was the unnamed whistleblower that crossed the headlines several years ago."

"You're speaking about Brad Johansson."

"Correct. I see you've done your homework. But that's how we knew the cancer drug trials were being stalled. And that the natural cures were being shunned, primarily because they can't be

patented. How do you patent broccoli, garlic, or onions? No patent—
no high-profit drugs for Big PhRMA. But Sorenson couldn't risk
transporting the cargo, so he arranged for Senator Lance to make
the delivery. The senator was a great supporter of our cause and
agreed. He believed his credentials made it safe for him to cross the
Mexican border to deliver the package initially. We're certain the
Consortium was involved in the series of mysterious deaths. You
believe it as well, but you're unable to prove it."

"How do you..."

"Please, let me continue. By some means, it was leaked that
Prince was conducting lab experiments with these amazing queen
bees, but incorrectly assumed he was trying to reproduce the
pill the Japanese have perfected with a protocol of high dosages
of propolis. A pill that has been proven to reverse the effects of
Alzheimer's and various cancers.

"You're referring to Dr. Mizukami. So, you don't want to
import the pills, because of what happened to Dr. Bradstreet and
others, but you want to produce your own?"

"You're partially correct. A string of holistic doctors who have
chosen to bring various drugs in from other countries illegally
to save their patients' lives—have lost their own lives. There are
approximately fifteen-point-five-million Americans living with
some form of cancer. More than a half million Americans a year
will die from these horrible diseases. The American Cancer Society
estimates another one-point-seven-million people will be diagnosed
with cancer this year alone. And these doctors apparently had the
cures. But we knew it would be virtually impossible to get FDA

approval for these remedies. We can barely skirt by with honey soap products that require FDA approval. So we devised another plan."

"I'm confused. Am I missing something? You *are* or *are not* going to try to reproduce Dr. Mizukami's pills?"

"Let me finish, my dear. It will become clear in a moment. Oliver Prince was a queen bee breeder and ran a small operation, so we had hoped he would stay off the radar. What he was attempting to do was to breed a colony of bees that could produce honey with exceedingly high levels of propolis to surpass the Japanese dosage. He succeeded."

Max heard mumbled bravos among the group, but continued to focus on the doctor.

"Each night, Oliver sent his latest lab results to our cloud. He sent his final notes the night before he was killed and his lab was raided. Luckily, he managed to scrub his hard drive before they arrived. The bees that you delivered will offer an opportunity to increase the strain in a certain segment of the honey bee populations in the US."

Max studied the cases. "Forgive me, but I still don't quite understand."

"I've been told that you are highly intelligent and resourceful. Please listen." Hal retrieved two large envelopes from the inside sleeve of each case and shook them a little. The sound was obviously of seeds.

"Baccharis dracunculifolia."

"Max, you exceed my expectations." He smiled, more to confer to the others he had chosen the right person for the mission. "Yes, these seeds will produce the only plant that these super bees will pollinate."

"But the plant is illegal in this country."

"For now, it's of minor consequence to us. We have people working on it, to get it legalized for other purposes, and not to draw attention to our own. In the meantime, the plants will grow among other vegetation and should not raise any red flags. I doubt the FDA will ever catch on—but the bees certainly will. Most importantly, through this pollination the bees will produce a super honey naturally. And, as I mentioned, far more potent than Dr. Mizukami's pills. Our super honey will contain the same natural vitamins, enzymes and phytonutrients that other raw, unpasteurized honeys possess. But it will also contain a high concentration of propolis, providing the highest level of anti-microbial activity, killing the cancer and stopping its growth." The doctor paused for a moment to measure whether Max was grasping the importance of what he was saying. Satisfied, he continued. "Our little super honey makers have the potential to make radiation and chemotherapy obsolete. No more unnecessary surgery. No more death. The fight to cure cancer—and I use the word *fight* loosely—is projected to be a one-hundred-seventy-three-billion-dollar industry by 2020. One that Big PhRMA will not surrender easily. Simply put, they can't afford to come up with a cure."

Sam was right again, Max thought, and then acknowledged, "That would be life-changing for certain, but I'm still unclear as to what your master plan is."

"I know this may appear to be a long shot, but our plan is well thought out. For over a year, we've collaborated with many established doctors and scientists—all who believe it is our best chance to eliminate cancer and other diseases. If we pull it off, the positive results will be staggering and will speak for themselves. At that juncture, it will be a hot button for any government official to try to shut down our operation."

"There are over three million colonies and one-hundred-thirty-five-thousand beekeepers. How can you be sure they'll all comply?" Max caught on, but was still skeptical.

"There are only five thousand beekeepers that take part in the USDA program. That's our focus group. I'm not saying there won't be other honeys on the market, but it will be up to our marketing campaign to steer people to this product. You see, cancer cells are obligate glucose metabolizers. They're compelled to absorb the glucose, and our super honey will become a Trojan horse laced with cancer-killing glucose. When the cancer cells gobble up the honey, it will eradicate the cancer. Our new super-honey protocol has even a greater effect in that it will also help to support healthy cells."

"And eventually, doctors will prescribe it to their patients."

"Hooray, Max. Now, you've got it! We have legions of enlightened doctors who will be including it in their patient regimen, unbeknownst to the FDA."

Pleased, Johnson was finally ready to lay out the specifics of the plan. "These men seated in this room are a select group of commercial beekeepers that have agreed to breed the colonies of super bees, along with the honey producers that will utilize the super bees to pollinate and produce the natural super honey. There are six species of honey bees that exist in the U.S. today and they will continue to pollinate the various flower crops that require them. We're merely creating a new species that will only be attracted to the propolis plant. With the drones and queens you delivered, we will be able to propagate six-hundred-thousand new colonies. One bee colony alone can produce a surplus of sixty to one hundred pounds of honey per year. Our conservative estimate is we'll be able to produce upwards of thirty-six-million pounds of super honey with high concentrations of propolis per year. When we are in full production, the members of the American Honey Producers Association and the American Beekeeping Federation, working outside this project, have pledged to cease making raw honey and focus solely on beeswax and cosmetic products. Once we make the switch, that's it."

"You referred to a marketing campaign."

"We're set to launch a campaign to revolutionize the way people think about honey. Every US citizen will be encouraged to include this highly potent, gooey syrup in their daily diets for nutritional value—on your toast, in your tea, or other food. It will take us a year before we're ready to go into full production with the new super raw honey products."

"What about the FDA?"

"If the campaign raises the FDA's awareness, we're prepared to invite them in to test our honey products for natural ingredients that we have already stocked on the shelves across the nation." The doctor beamed.

It was clear to all in the room that he was proud of the ingenious deception.

"But in a year's time, when we start to substitute the existing honey products, cereals, et cetera, and restock with our super honey, it will be hard for them to decipher. It will still be raw natural honey with no additives. The only difference is, it will be a lifesaving formula, under the radar of our friends at the FDA. By the time we make the switch, they won't even take notice. Those afflicted with cancer and other diseases will stave off or reverse the life-threatening negative affects right under their government's nose. Dramatic results in the US populations' health will begin to show within a relatively short period. And years from now, when cancer is eradicated, the FDA and Big PhRMA will be at a loss for an explanation."

"This is incredible—brilliant, actually! But I have one remaining question. Why are you trusting me with this information?"

"Max, we've followed your progress on this case and you've done an exemplary job. Aside from Sorenson, we have other known sources reporting that the FDA is purposely dragging their feet at producing similar medication, while knowing the current drugs and treatments only attack the symptoms of cancer. Your efforts have put Big PhRMA and the FDA on the president's watch list, doing a great service to those in the alternative and holistic fields of medicine." The doctor paused for a moment, giving Max an opportunity to absorb the gravity of his comment. After gauging her expression, he continued. "With full candor, we need someone on the outside. Someone in the driver's seat with your skills and connections should anything happen to any of us. We place our full trust in you and that you'll get the truth to the right people—should it be necessary."

Max hesitated. It was hard to ignore all the eyes upon her looking for agreement. "I'm not flattered with this new responsibility—but you can trust that your secret is safe with me."

"And you have our word that no one will ever know this meeting took place," Hal assured. "Or even that Max Ford had visited our great State of Texas."

Feeling an unexplained sense of relief, she quipped, "And I thought the FDA was in control." A smile crossed her lips.

Hal mirrored her expression. "You have to admit; it is a sweet revenge." He then held out an envelope.

"What's that?" Max asked.

"It contains the proof you need to connect the Consortium with Big PhRMA."

All those at the table stood and gave a hearty applause in Max's direction.

Half-way into the jubilation, the applause came to a sudden stop. A loud explosion shook the room. Then another. Everyone leaped up and ran to the windows. Everyone except Max who stood frozen in place. It was not from fear; it was instinct.

"Down everyone!" shouted one of the members.

A third disastrous explosion sent a barrage of debris and flying glass through the large windows, spewing threatening materials in every direction. Minutes later, dazed moans resonated among the dust-filled room, along with an ominous buzzing hum. A few seconds later, Max heard a bellowing voice cry out to everyone asking if they were okay. One by one, the weak but able voices returned a welcomed confirmation. Then, the same voice called for help. As best Max could determine, he was somewhere near where the large conference table was previously located. Edging out from under the rubble, Max managed to stand upright and clawed her way through the debris, working toward his desperate call. There, lying under a stack of broken chairs was Dr. Harold Johnson. He was badly wounded, but was still grasping tightly to the envelope containing the evidence.

"Max, be careful. The Consortium doesn't fail often."

The building across the street, marked with the number 3666, was completely demolished.

Author's Note

The Beekeeper's Secret is a fictional tale laced with incredible, sometimes disturbing, but eye-opening facts in the public domain about our healthcare industry and about truth in advertising. The principal characters and many of the locations are fictitious. All reference to the American Beekeeping Federation and the American Honey Producers Association are pure fiction and crafted by the author. There may appear to be a tinge of conspiracy surrounding the deaths of more than eighty holistic doctors, but it is meant to challenge the reader to question the events put forward. In all cases, where numerous real people were mentioned, both living and deceased, every attempt to honor and show respect was paramount.

Given one of the main threads, it is also not the author's intent to discourage the reader from traditional medicine, but to bring awareness to the various alternative methods available today. However, in a world where it has becoming increasingly important to trust, then verify, the wealth of information available today should be used with caution. But it provides an excellent source to engender questions when seeking the right course of treatment.

And when it comes to managing one's healthcare, a second, third or fourth opinion, if necessary, should be sought. It is important to remember that we are the consumer and those in the medical field are there to serve us.

A final takeaway is that we don't rent our bodies—we own them for life. This cautionary cliché, *you are what you eat*, is more than a platitude. It could be a lifesaver.

Acknowledgments

The Editor: After the completion of each novel I'm faced with a dilemma. How to recognize someone who has had the greatest impact in the creation of the novel. After using the Dedication and the Acknowledgment in past novels, it never appeared sufficient. Joe Fernandez, my loving husband, avid supporter, and incredible substantive editor, deserves the highest recognition. After 39 years together, he made it possible for me to embark on this amazing journey as an author; to produce entertaining, intellectual, and informative novels. His literary contributions alone are invaluable. Additionally, his diligent, in-depth editing enhances my narrative. His scrutiny of segueways, nuances, facts, and the content that assures plausibility, is priceless. My mantra has become, "If Joe doesn't get it, neither will the reader." Because of him, my writing style has improved immensely, and because of him I've written six novels of which I am proud. Perhaps, the only place to fully appreciate the sacrifices he has made is in that special place in my heart that he occupies.

The Publisher: Both Joe and I offer our deep appreciation to my publisher, David Dunham, for his continued confidence in me as a novelist. And for giving of his own time to see my projects to fruition. But I know David could not do it without his amazing colleagues and support team of editors and designers. Thanks to all of you.

The Alpha/Beta Readers: Our profound thanks go to my special inner circle of talented readers whose objective insights and valuable feedback from various perspectives continue to help enrich my stories. It's amazing after the number of rereads and edits Joe and I run the manuscript through, this group still finds the nagging oversights and offer helpful hints: to Kenney DeCamp, Michael DeStefano, Debbie Dunham, Richard Halpern, Ann Howells, Donna Post, Alfredo Vedro.

The Fact Checkers: A special thanks goes to those who have graciously given their time to conduct a fact-check review of critical portions of the manuscript for accuracy in their field of expertise: Gene Brandi, Gene Brandi Apiaries, Past President of American Beekeeping Federation, Dr. Kenneth D. Henson, MD, FACC, Tom Wysmuller, NASA Apollo Era (Ret.), VP Medical Claims Operations, Phoenix Mutual Life Insurance Company (Former).

Family and Friends: Lastly, I am indebted to all my family and friends from around the world, too numerous to mention, for all the love and support they have given me throughout this endeavor.

About The Author

*Photo by
Giovanni Lunardi,
Photographer*

If you relish suspense thrillers with a tinge of conspiracy, you'll enjoy Sally Fernandez' novels. Readers have said she pens riveting plots of intrigue and political awakening, seamlessly blending fact with fiction…or fiction with fact…you be the judge.

As a novelist of provocative political thrillers steeped in facts, she wasn't always twisting facts with fiction. Heavily endowed with skills acquired in banking, she embarked on her writing career. Her focus on computer technology, business consulting, and project management, enhanced by business and technical writing, proved to be a boon. Her books of fiction also reflect the knowledge garnered from her business experiences, while living in New York City, San Francisco, and Hong Kong.

Sally's foray into writing fiction officially began in 2007 when the presidential election cycle was in full swing. The overwhelming political spin by the media compelled her to question the frightening possibilities the political scene could generate. As a confirmed political junkie, she took to the keyboard armed with unwinding events and discovered a new and exciting career.

The Beekeeper's Secret is her sixth novel and the second in the "Max Ford Thriller" series, preceded by *Climatized*, featuring Maxine Ford as the female protagonist. Sally's prior series, "The Simon Tetralogy," is comprised of *Brotherhood Beyond the Yard*, *Noble's Quest*, *The Ultimate Revenge* and *Redemption*. Each book provides an exhilarating platform for the next, with a gripping narrative that challenges the reader to put the book down. The ever-elusive Simon's daring escapes in the preceding novels, allow him to add unheard of dimensions that provide intrigue to hold the reader. Her development of the other characters has created a lasting bond between them and the reader, especially now that Max has taken center stage.

As a world traveler, Sally has visited every continent and over fifty countries. Her adventure travels with her husband include a scientific expedition in Antarctica, four African safaris, archaeological digs in Majorca and Peru, along with high-altitude treks in Bhutan, Tibet, and Mongolia. Sally and her husband, also the editor-in-residence, continue to travel extensively throughout the world.

Climatized:
A Max Ford Thriller

"Never will you be forced to the edge of your seat in a mystery thriller while being steeped in scientific education of great importance to humanity."

—Dr. Jay Lehr, Science Director of The Heartland Institute

"...a murder-mystery thriller, full of political intrigue and meticulous scientific accuracy, that gets about as close as you can get to the truth...and still call it fiction."

—Dr. Harold Doiron, Chairman, The Right Climate Stuff research team

"In *Climatized*, Sally Fernandez has deftly created a novel out of perhaps the biggest deception in the history of the Modern World..."

—Dennis T. Avery, New York Times Bestselling Co-Author of Unstoppable Global Warming: Every 1,500 Years

After resigning her post at the States Intelligence Agency, Maxine Ford declares her independence as she bursts on to the Washington scene as a private investigator. She displays her usual no-holds-barred style, showing no obeisance to the elite politicians. Right out of the starting gate, she finds herself in the cauldron of mystery, murder, and mayhem. All of her clients are warned to prepare themselves for the truth…at all costs. Max is hired by the wife of a prominent senator to determine the cause of his untimely death. It leads her to discover that three world-renowned scientists had been killed days before they were scheduled to testify before the late senator's investigative committee. Meanwhile, a fourth scientist has gone missing. Max determined he is the key to unearthing the motives behind the deaths. Following the many twists and turns, Max and her associate, Jackson Monroe uncover a powerful organization responsible for the killings.

Fernandez' crackerjack international thriller once again expertly weaves fact with fiction. The readers will be beguiled by the artistic marriage of established facts with a storyline that lifts creativity to new heights. A classic blend of character study and well-plotted action sequences keeps the pages turning faster and faster. A hair-raising page-turner from start to finish.

The Simon Tetralogy

Brotherhood Beyond the Yard (published in 2011) is an international thriller that takes readers from the streets of Florence, Italy to the highest seats of power in Washington D.C. It was the first in what was to become a series titled "The Simon Tetralogy." The story introduces the enigmatic Simon Hall, a man best described 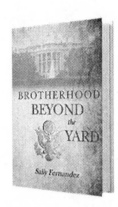 as a cross between Brad Pitt's character in *Meet Joe Black* and Leonardo DiCaprio's character in *Catch Me If You Can.*

As the leader of a group of scholars known as *La Fratellanza* (The Brotherhood), Simon brings an intellectual game into real life by involving the election of a president, the banking crisis and international terrorism.

The second installment **Noble's Quest,** introduces another level of intrigue with intoxicating twists and turns. But the hunt for Simon continues. **The Ultimate Revenge** brings an explosive conclusion to what was supposed to be the trilogy, but questions were left unanswered. **Redemption** continues to lead the reader

through horrifying events until the country is saved from an economic crisis that would resonate around the world.

Throughout the tetralogy, the hunt for Simon never ceases as he continues to unleash diabolical plots in the US and abroad. The readers and the characters are led first to admire him and then slowly grow to fear him. The readers will be beguiled by the artistic marriage of established facts with a storyline that lifts creativity to new heights. Readers are also challenged to separate fact from fiction, giving rise to the question, **WHAT IF?**

The tale begins...